Ali[illegible] minister, was[illegible] in the Sco[illegible] age of eigh[illegible] Royal Navy; two-and-a-half years spent aboard a cruiser was later to give him the background for HMS *Ulysses*, his first novel, the outstanding documentary novel on the war at sea. After the war, he gained an English Honours degree at Glasgow University, and became a schoolmaster. In 1983 he was awarded a D.Litt from the same university.

By the early 1970s he was one of the top 10 bestselling authors in the world, and the biggest-selling Briton. He wrote twenty-nine worldwide bestsellers that have sold more than 30 million copies, and many of which have been filmed, including *The Guns of Navarone, Where Eagles Dare, Fear is the Key* and *Ice Station Zebra*. He is now recognized as one of the outstanding popular writers of the 20th century. Alistair MacLean died in 1987 at his home in Switzerland.

By Alistair MacLean

HMS Ulysses
The Guns of Navarone
South by Java Head
The Last Frontier
Night Without End
Fear is the Key
The Dark Crusader
The Satan Bug
The Golden Rendezvous
Ice Station Zebra
When Eight Bells Toll
Where Eagles Dare
Force 10 from Navarone
Puppet on a Chain
Caravan to Vaccarès
Bear Island
The Way to Dusty Death
Breakheart Pass
Circus
The Golden Gate
Seawitch
Goodbye California
Athabasca
River of Death
Partisans
Floodgate
San Andreas
The Lonely Sea (stories)
Santorini

ALISTAIR MACLEAN

The Way to Dusty Death

HARPER

Harper
An imprint of HarperCollins*Publishers*
77–85 Fulham Palace Road,
Hammersmith, London W6 8JB

www.harpercollins.co.uk

This paperback edition 2009
1

First published in Great Britain by
William Collins Sons & Co. Ltd 1973
then in paperback by Fontana 1975

A catalogue record for this book is available from the British Library

ISBN 978-0-00-785178-2

Typeset in Meridien by Thomson Digital, India

Printed and bound in Great Britain by
Clays Ltd, St Ives plc

To Mary Marcelle

CHAPTER ONE

Harlow sat by the side of the race-track on that hot and cloudless afternoon, his long hair blowing about in the fresh breeze and partially obscuring his face, his golden helmet clutched so tightly in his gauntleted hands that he appeared to be trying to crush it: the hands were shaking uncontrollably and occasional violent tremors racked his entire body.

His own car, from which he had been miraculously thrown clear, uninjured, just before it had overturned lay, of all places, in its own Coronado pits, upside down and with its wheels spinning idly. Wisps of smoke were coming from an engine already engulfed under a mound of foam from the fire extinguishers and it was clear that there was now little danger of an explosion from the unruptured fuel tanks.

Alexis Dunnet, the first to reach Harlow, noticed that he wasn't looking at his own car but was staring trance-like at a spot about two hundred yards farther along the track where an already dead man called Isaac Jethou was being cremated in the white-flamed funeral pyre of what had once been his Grand Prix Formula One racing car. There was curiously little smoke coming from the blazing wreck, presumably because of the intense heat given off by the incandescent magnesium alloy wheels, and when the gusting wind occasionally parted the towering curtains of flame Jethou could be seen sitting bolt upright in his cockpit, the one apparently undamaged structure left in an otherwise shattered and unrecognizable mass of twisted steel: at least Dunnet *knew* it was Jethou but what he was seeing was a blackened and horribly charred remnant of a human being.

The many thousands of people in the stands and lining the track were motionless and soundless, staring in transfixed and incredulous awe and horror at the burning car. The last of the engines of the Grand Prix cars – there were nine of them stopped in sight of the pits, some drivers standing by their sides – died away as the race marshals frantically flagged the abandonment of the race.

The public address system had fallen silent now, as did a siren's ululating wail as an ambulance screeching to a halt at a prudent distance from Jethou's car, its flashing light fading into nothingness against the white blaze in the background. Rescue workers in aluminium asbestos suits, some operating giant wheeled fire-extinguishers, some armed with crowbars and axes, were trying desperately, for some reason wholly beyond the bounds of logic, to get sufficiently close to the car to drag the cindered corpse free, but the undiminished intensity of the flames made a mockery of their desperation. Their efforts were as futile as the presence of the ambulance was unnecessary. Jethou was beyond any mortal help or hope.

Dunnet looked away and down at the overalled figure beside him. The hands that held the golden helmet still trembled unceasingly and the eyes still fixed immovably on the sheeted flames that now quite enveloped Isaac Jethou's car were the eyes of an eagle gone blind. Dunnet reached for his shoulder and shook it gently but he paid no heed. Dunnet asked him if he were hurt for his face and trembling hands were masked in blood: he had cart-wheeled at least half a dozen times after being thrown from his car in the final moments before it had upended and come to rest in its own pits. Harlow stirred and looked at Dunnet, blinking, like a man slowly arousing himself from a nightmare, then shook his head.

Two ambulance men with a stretcher came towards them at a dead run, but Harlow, unaided except for Dunnet's supporting hand under his upper arm, pushed himself shakily to his feet and waved them off. He didn't, however, seem to object to what little help Dunnet's hand lent him and they walked slowly back to the Coronado pits, the still dazed and virtually uncomprehending Harlow, Dunnet tall, thin, with dark hair parted in the middle, a dark pencil-line moustache and rimless glasses, everyone's idealized conception of a city accountant even though his passport declared him to be a journalist.

MacAlpine, a fire-extinguisher still held in one hand, turned to meet them at the entrance to the pits. James MacAlpine, owner and manager of the Coronado racing team, dressed in a now stained tan gaberdine suit, was in his mid-fifties, as heavily jowled as he was heavily built and had a deeply lined face under an impressive mane of black and silver hair. Behind him, Jacobson, the chief mechanic and his two red-haired assistants, the Rafferty twins who for some reason unknown were invariably referred to as Tweedledum and Tweedledee, still ministered to the smouldering Coronado, while behind the car two other men, white-coated first-aid men, were carrying out more serious ministrations of their own: on the ground, unconscious but still clutching the pad and pencil with which she had been taking lap times, lay Mary MacAlpine, the owner's black-haired, twenty-year-old daughter. The first-aid men were bent over her left leg and scissoring open to the knee wine-red slacks that had been white moments ago. MacAlpine took Harlow's arm, deliberately shielding him from the sight of his daughter, and led him to the little shelter behind the pits. MacAlpine was an extremely able, competent and tough man, as millionaires tend to be: beneath the toughness, as of now, lay a kindness and depth of consideration of which no one would have dared to accuse him.

In the back of the shelter stood a small wooden crate which was, in effect, a portable bar. Most of it was given over to an ice-box stocked with a little beer and lots of soft drinks, chiefly for the mechanics, for working under that torrid sun was thirsty business. There were also two bottles of champagne for it had not been unreasonable to expect of a man who had just reeled off a near-impossible five consecutive Grand Prix victories that he might just possibly achieve his sixth. Harlow opened the lid of the crate, ignored the ice-box, lifted out a bottle of brandy and half-filled the tumbler, the neck of the bottle chattering violently against the rim of the glass: more brandy spilled to the ground than went into the glass. He required both hands to lift the glass to his mouth and now the rim of the tumbler, castanet-like fashion, struck up an even more erratic tattoo against his teeth than the bottle had on the glass. He managed to get some of it down but most of the glass's contents overflowed by the two sides of his mouth, coursed down the blood-streaked chin to stain the white racing overalls to exactly the same colour as the slacks of the injured girl outside. Harlow stared bemusedly at the empty glass, sank on to a bench and reached for the bottle again.

MacAlpine looked at Dunnet, his face without expression. Harlow had suffered three major crashes in his racing career, in the last of which, two years previously, he had sustained near-fatal injuries: on that last occasion, he had been smiling, albeit in agony, as his stretcher had been loaded aboard the ambulance plane for the flight back to London and the left hand he had used to give the thumbs-up signal – his right forearm had been broken in two places – had been as steady as if graven from marble. But more dismaying was the fact that apart from a token sip of celebration champagne he had never touched hard alcohol in his life.

It happens to them all, MacAlpine had always maintained, sooner or later it happens to them all. No matter how cool or brave or brilliant they were, it happened to them all, and the more steely their icy calm and control the more fragile it was. MacAlpine was never a man to be averse to the odd hyperbolic turn of phrase and there was a handful – but only a handful – of outstanding ex-Grand Prix drivers around who had retired at the top of their physical and mental form, sufficient, at any rate, to disprove MacAlpine's statement in its entirety. But it was well enough known that there existed top-flight drivers who had crashed or who had suffered so much nervous and mental fatigue that they had become empty shells of their former selves, that there were among the current twenty-four Grand Prix drivers four or five who would never win a race again because they had no intention of ever trying to do so, who kept going only in order to shore up the façade of a now empty pride.

But there are some things that are not done in the racing world and one of those is that you don't remove a man from the Grand Prix roster just because his nerve is gone.

But that MacAlpine was more often right than wrong was sadly clear from the sight of that trembling figure hunched on the bench. If ever a man had gone over the top, had reached and passed the limit of endurance before tumbling over the precipice of self-abnegation and hapless acceptance of ultimate defeat, it was Johnny Harlow, the golden boy of the Grand Prix circuits, unquestionably, until that afternoon, the outstanding driver of his time and, it was being increasingly suggested, of all time: with last year's world championship safely his and the current year's, by any reasonable standards, almost inevitably his with half the Grand Prix races still to run, Harlow's will and nerve would have appeared to have crumbled beyond recovery: it was plain to MacAlpine and Dunnet that the charred being who had been Isaac Jethou would haunt him for however long his days were to be.

Not that the signs hadn't been there before for those with eyes to see them and most of the drivers and mechanics on the circuits had the kind of eyes that were required. Ever since the second Grand Prix race of the season, which he had easily and convincingly won unaware of the fact that his brilliant younger brother had been forced off the track and had telescoped his car into a third of its length against the base of a pine tree at something over a hundred and fifty miles an hour, the signs had been there. Never a sociable or gregarious person, he had become increasingly withdrawn, increasingly taciturn and when he smiled, and it was rarely, it was the empty smile of a man who could find nothing in life to smile about. Normally the most icily calculating and safety-conscious of drivers, his impeccable standards had become eroded and his previous near obsession with safety dismayingly decreased while, contradictorily, he had consistently kept on breaking lap records on circuits throughout Europe. But he had continued on his record-breaking way, capturing one Grand Prix trophy after the other at the increasingly mounting expense of himself and his fellow competitors: his driving had become reckless and increasingly dangerous and the other drivers, tough and hardened professionals though they all were, began to go in fear of him for instead of disputing a corner with him as they would normally have done they had nearly all of them fallen into the habit of pulling well in when they saw his lime-green Coronado closing up on their driving mirrors. This, in all conscience, was seldom enough, for Harlow had an extremely simple race-winning formula – to get in front and stay there.

By now more and more people were saying out loud that his suicidally competitive driving on the racetracks signified not a battle against his peers but a battle against himself. It had become increasingly obvious, latterly painfully obvious, that this was one battle that he would never win, that this last ditch stand against his failing nerve could have only one end, that one day his luck would run out. And so it had, and so had Isaac Jethou's, and Johnny Harlow, for all the world to see, had lost his last battle on the Grand Prix tracks of Europe and America. Maybe he would move out on the tracks again, maybe he would start fighting again: but it seemed certain then that no one knew with more dreadful clarity than Harlow that his fighting days were over.

For a third time Harlow reached out for the neck of the brandy bottle, his hands as unsteady as ever. The once-full bottle was now one-third empty but only a fraction of that had found its way down his throat, so uncontrollable were his movements. MacAlpine looked gravely at Dunnet, shrugged his heavy shoulders in a gesture of either resignation or acceptance and then glanced out into the pits. An ambulance had just arrived for his daughter and as MacAlpine hurried out Dunnet set about cleaning up Harlow's face with the aid of a sponge and a bucket of water. Harlow didn't seem to care one way or another whether his face was washed: whatever his thoughts were, and in the circumstances it would have taken an idiot not to read them aright, his entire attention appeared to be concentrated on the contents of that bottle of Martell, the picture of a man, if ever there was one, who desperately needed and urgently sought immediate oblivion.

It was as well, perhaps, that both Harlow and MacAlpine failed to notice a person standing just outside the door whose expression clearly indicated that he would take quite some pleasure in assisting Harlow into a state of permanent oblivion. Rory, MacAlpine's son, a dark curly-haired youth of a normally amiable, even sunny, disposition had now a dark thundercloud on his face, an unthinkable expression for one who for years, and until only a few minutes previously, regarded Harlow as the idol of his life. Rory looked away towards the ambulance where his unconscious and blood-soaked sister lay and then the unthinkable was no longer so. He turned again to look at Harlow and now the emotion reflected in his eyes was as close to outright hatred as a sixteen-year-old was ever likely to achieve.

The official inquiry into the cause of the accident, held almost immediately afterwards, predictably failed to indict any one man as the sole cause of the disaster. Official race inquiries almost never did, including the notorious inquiry into that unparalleled Le Mans holocaust when seventy-three spectators were killed and no one was found to blame whereas it was common knowledge at the time that one man and one man only – dead now these many years – had been the person responsible for it.

This particular inquiry failed to indict, in spite of the fact that two or three thousand people in the main stands would unhesitatingly have laid the sole charge at the door of Johnny Harlow. But even more damning was the incontrovertible evidence supplied in the small hall where the inquiry was held by a TV playback of the entire incident. The projection screen had been small and stained but the picture clear enough and the sound effects all too vivid and true to life. In the re-run of the film – it lasted barely twenty seconds but was screened five times – three Grand Prix cars, viewed from the rear but being closely followed by the telescopic zoom lens, could be seen approaching the pits. Harlow, in his Coronado, was closing up on the leading car, a vintage privately-entered Ferrari that was leading only by virtue of the fact that it had already lost a lap. Moving even more quickly than Harlow and well clear on the other side of the track was a works-entered fire-engine-red Ferrari driven by a brilliant Californian, Isaac Jethou. In the straight Jethou's twelve cylinders had a considerable edge over Harlow's eight and it was clear that he intended to pass. It seemed that Harlow, too, was quite aware of this for his brake lights came on in keeping with his apparent intention of easing slightly and tucking in behind the slower car while Jethou swept by.

Suddenly, incredibly, Harlow's brake lights went out and the Coronado swerved violently outwards as if Harlow had decided he could overtake the car in front before Jethou could overtake him. If that had been his inexplicable intention then it had been the most foolhardy of his life, for he had taken his car directly into the path of Isaac Jethou who, on that straight, could not have been travelling at less than 180 miles an hour and who, in the fraction of the second available to him, had never even the most remote shadow of a chance to take the only braking or avoiding action that could have saved him.

At the moment of impact, Jethou's front wheel struck squarely into the side of Harlow's front wheel. For Harlow, the consequences of the collision were, in all conscience, serious enough for it sent his car into an uncontrollable spin, but for Jethou they were disastrous. Even above the cacophonous clamour of engines under maximum revolutions and the screeching of locked tyres on the tarmac, the bursting of Jethou's front tyre was heard as a rifle shot and from that instant Jethou was a dead man. His Ferrari, wholly out of control and now no more than a mindless mechanical monster bent on its own destruction, smashed into and caromed off the nearside safety barrier and, already belching gouts of red flame and black oily smoke, careered wildly across the track to strike the far side barrier, rear end first, at a speed of still over a hundred miles an hour. The Ferrari, spinning wildly, slid down the track for about two hundred yards, turned over twice and came to rest on all four wrecked wheels, Jethou still trapped in the cockpit but even then almost certainly dead. It was then that the red flames turned to white.

That Harlow had been directly responsible for Jethou's death was beyond dispute but Harlow, with eleven Grand Prix wins behind him in seventeen months was, by definition and on his record, the best driver in the world and one simply does not indict the best driver in the world. It is not the done thing. The whole tragic affair was attributed to the race-track equivalent of an act of God and the curtain was discreetly lowered to indicate the end of the act.

CHAPTER TWO

The French, even at their most relaxed and unemotional, are little given to hiding their feelings and the packed crowd at Clermont-Ferrand that day, which was notably unrelaxed and highly emotional, was in no mood to depart from their Latin norm. As Harlow, head bowed, trudged rather than walked along the side of the Coronado pits, they became very vocal indeed. Their booing, hissing, cat-calling and just plain shouts of anger, accompanied by much Gallic waving of clenched fists, was as threatening as it was frightening. Not only was it an ugly scene, it was one that looked as if it would only require one single flash-point to trigger off a near riot, to convert their vengeful emotions towards Johnny Harlow into physical action against him and this, it was clear, was the apprehension that was uppermost in the minds of the police, for they moved in close to afford Harlow such protection as he might require. It was equally clear from the expressions on their faces that the police did not relish their task, and from the way they averted their faces from Harlow that they sympathized with their countrymen's feelings.

A few paces behind Harlow, flanked by Dunnet and MacAlpine, walked another man who clearly shared the opinions of police and spectators. Angrily twirling his racing helmet by its strap, he was clad in racing overalls identical to those that Harlow was wearing: Nicolo Tracchia was, in fact, the No. 2 driver in the Coronado racing team. Tracchia was almost outrageously handsome, with dark curling hair, a gleaming perfection of teeth that no dentifrice manufacturer would ever dare use as an advertisement and a sun-tan that would have turned a life-guard pale green. That he wasn't looking particularly happy at that moment was directly attributable to the fact that he was scowling heavily: the legendary Tracchia scowl was a memorable thing of wonder, in constant use and held in differing degrees of respect, awe and downright fear but never ignored. Tracchia had a low opinion of his fellow-man and regarded the majority of people, and this with particular reference to his fellow Grand Prix drivers, as retarded adolescents.

Undcrstandably, hc opcratcd in a limitcd social circle. What made matters worse for Tracchia was his realization that, brilliant driver though he was, he was fractionally less good than Harlow, and even this was exacerbated by the knowledge that, no matter how long or desperately he tried, he would never quite close that fractional gap. When he spoke now to MacAlpine he made no effort to lower his voice which in the circumstances mattered not at all for Harlow could not possibly have heard him above the baying of the crowd: but it was quite clear that Tracchia would not have lowered his voice no matter what the circumstances.

'An act of God!' The bitter incredulity in the voice was wholly genuine. 'Jesus Christ! Did you hear what those cretins called it? An act of God! An act of murder, I call it.'

'No, lad, no.' MacAlpine put his hand on Tracchia's shoulder, only to have it angrily shrugged off. MacAlpine sighed. 'At the very outside, manslaughter. And not even that. You know yourself how many Grand Prix drivers have died in the past four years because their cars went wild.'

'Wild! Wild!' Tracchia, at a momentary and most uncharacteristic loss for words, gazed heavenwards in silent appeal. 'Good God, Mac, we all saw it on the screen. We saw it five times. He took his foot off the brake and pulled out straight in front of Jethou. An act of God! Sure, sure, sure. It's an act of God because he's won eleven Grand Prix in seventeen months, because he won last year's championship and looks as if he's going to do the same this year.'

'What do you mean?'

'You know damn well what I mean. Take him off the tracks and you might as well take us all off the tracks. He's the champion, isn't he? If he's that bad, then what the hell must the rest of us be like? We know that's not the case, but will the public? Will they hell. God knows that there are already too many people, and damned influential people as well, agitating that Grand Prix racing should be banned throughout the world, and too many countries just begging for a good excuse to get out. This would be the excuse of a lifetime. We *need* our Johnny Harlows, don't we, Mac? Even though they do go around killing people.'

'I thought he was your friend, Nikki?'

'Sure, Mac. Sure he's my friend. So was Jethou.'

There was no reply for MacAlpine to make to this so he made none. Tracchia appeared to have said his say, for he fell silent and got back to his scowling. In silence and in safety – the police escort had been steadily increasing – the four men reached the Coronado pits. Without a glance at or word to anyone Harlow made for the little shelter at the rear of the pits. In their turn nobody – Jacobson and his two mechanics were there also – made any attempt either to speak to or stop him, nor did any among them do even as much as trouble to exchange significant glances: the starkly obvious requires no emphasis. Jacobson ignored him entirely and came up to MacAlpine. The chief mechanic – and he was one of acknowledged genius – was a lean, tall and strongly built man. He had a dark and deeply lined face that looked as if it hadn't smiled for a long time and wasn't about to make an exception in this case either.

He said: 'Harlow's clear, of course.'

'Of course? I don't understand.'

'*I* have to tell *you*? Indict Harlow and you set the sport back ten years. Too many millions tied up in it to allow that to happen. Isn't there now, Mr MacAlpine?'

MacAlpine looked at him reflectively, not answering, glanced briefly at the still scowling Tracchia, turned away and walked across to Harlow's battered and fire-blistered Coronado which was by that time back on all four wheels. He examined it leisurely, almost contemplatively, stooped over the cockpit, turned the steering wheel which offered no resistance to his hand, then straightened.

He said: 'Well, now. I wonder.'

Jacobson looked at him coldly. His eyes, expressing displeasure, could be as formidable and intimidating as Tracchia's scowl. He said: '*I* prepared that car, Mr MacAlpine.'

MacAlpine's shoulders rose and fell in a long moment of silence.

'I know, Jacobson, I know. I also know you're the best in the business. I also know that you've been too long in it to talk nonsense. *Any* car can go. How long?'

'You want me to start now?'

'That's it.'

'Four hours.' Jacobson was curt, offence given and taken. 'Six at the most.'

MacAlpine nodded, took Dunnet by the arm, prepared to walk away, then halted. Tracchia and Rory were together talking in low indistinct voices but their words didn't have to be understood, the rigid hostility in their expressions as they looked at Harlow and his bottle of brandy inside the hut were eloquent enough. MacAlpine, his hand still on Dunnet's arm, moved away and sighed again.

'Johnny's not making too many friends today, is he?'

'He hasn't been for far too many days. And I think that here's another friend that he's about not to make.'

'Oh Jesus.' Sighs seemed to be becoming second nature to MacAlpine. 'Neubauer does seem to have something on his mind.'

The figure in sky-blue racing overalls striding towards the pits did indeed seem to have something on his mind. Neubauer was tall, very blond and completely Nordic in appearance although he was in fact Austrian. The No. 1 driver for team Cagliari – he had the word *Cagliari* emblazoned across the chest of his overalls – his consistent brilliance on the Grand Prix tracks had made him the acknowledged crown prince of racing and Harlow's eventual and inevitable successor. Like Tracchia, he was a cool, distant man wholly incapable of standing fools at any price, far less gladly. Like Tracchia, his friends and intimates were restricted to a very small group indeed: it was a matter for neither wonder nor speculation that those two men, the most unforgiving of rivals on the race-tracks were, off-duty, close friends.

Neubauer, with compressed lips and cold pale-blue eyes glittering, was clearly a very angry man and his humour wasn't improved when MacAlpine moved his massive bulk to block his way. Neubauer had no option other than to stop: big man though he was MacAlpine was very much bigger. When he spoke it was with his teeth clamped together.

'Out of my way.'

MacAlpine looked at him in mild surprise.

'You said what?'

'Sorry, Mr MacAlpine. Where's that bastard Harlow?'

'Leave him be. He's not well.'

'And Jethou is, I suppose? I don't know who the hell or what the hell Harlow is or is supposed to be and I don't care. Why should that maniac get off scot-free? He *is* a maniac. You know it. We all know it. He forced me off the road twice today, that could just as well have been me burnt to death as Jethou. I'm giving you warning, Mr MacAlpine. I'm going to call a meeting of the GPDA and have him banned from the circuits.'

'You're the last person who can afford to do that, Willi.' MacAlpine put his hands on Neubauer's shoulders. 'The last person who can afford to put the finger on Johnny. If Harlow goes, who's the next champion?'

Neubauer stared at him. Some of the fury left his face and he stared at MacAlpine in almost bewildered disbelief. When his voice came it was low, almost an uncertain whisper. 'You think I would do it for that, Mr MacAlpine?'

'No, Willi, I don't. I'm just pointing out that most others would.'

There was a long pause during which what was left of Neubauer's anger died away. He said quietly: 'He's a killer. He'll kill again.' Gently, he removed MacAlpine's hands, turned and left the pits. Thoughtfully, worriedly Dunnet watched him leave.

'He could be right, James. Sure, sure, he's won five Grand Prix in a row but ever since his brother was killed in the Spanish Grand Prix – well, you know.'

'Five Grand Prix under his belt and you're trying to tell me that his nerve is gone?'

'I don't know what's gone. I just don't know. All I know is that the safest driver on the circuits has become so reckless and dangerous, so suicidally competitive if you like, that the other drivers are just plain scared of him. As far as they are concerned, the freedom of the road is his, they'd rather live than dispute a yard of track with him. *That's* why he keeps on winning.'

MacAlpine regarded Dunnet closely and shook his head in unease. He, MacAlpine, and not

Dunnet, was the acknowledged expert, but MacAlpine held Dunnet and his opinions in the highest regard. Dunnet was an extraordinarily shrewd, intelligent and able person. He was a journalist by profession, and a highly competent one, who had switched from being a political analyst to a sports commentator for the admittedly unarguable reason that there is no topic on earth so irretrievably dull as politics. The acute penetration and remarkable powers of observation and analysis that had made him so formidable a figure on the Westminster scene he had transferred easily and successfully to the race-tracks of the world. A regular correspondent for a British national daily and two motoring magazines, one British, one American – although he did a remarkable amount of freelance work on the side – he had rapidly established himself as one of the very few really outstanding motor racing journalists in the world. To do this in the space of just over two years had been a quite outstanding achievement by any standard. So successful had he been, indeed, that he had incurred the envy and displeasure, not to say the outright wrath, of a considerable number of his less gifted peers.

Nor was their minimal regard for him in any way heightened by what they sourly regarded as the limpet-like persistency with which he had attached himself to the Coronado team on an almost permanent basis. Not that there were any laws, written or unwritten, about this sort of behaviour, for no independent journalist had ever done this sort of thing before. Now that it had been done it was, his fellow-writers said, a thing that simply was not done. It was his job, they maintained and complained, to write in a fair and unbiased fashion on *all* the cars and *all* the drivers in the Grand Prix field and their resentment remained undiminished when he pointed out to them, reasonably and with unchallengeable accuracy, that this was precisely what he did. What really grieved them, of course, was that he had the inside track on the Coronado team, then the fastest burgeoning and most glamorous race company in the business: and it would have been difficult to deny that the number of off-track articles he had written partly about the team but primarily about Harlow would have made up a pretty fair-size volume. Nor had matters been helped by the existence of a book on which he had collaborated with Harlow.

MacAlpine said: 'I'm afraid you're right, Alexis. Which means that I know you're right but I don't even want to admit it to myself. He's just terrifying the living daylights out of everyone. And out of me. And now this.'

They looked across the pits to where Harlow was sitting on a bench just outside the shelter. Uncaring whether he was observed or not, he half-filled a glass from a rapidly diminishing brandy bottle. One did not have to have eyesight to know that the hands were still shaking:

diminishing though the protesting roar of the crowd still was, it was still sufficient to make normal conversation difficult: nevertheless, the castanet rattle of glass against glass could be clearly heard. Harlow took a quick gulp from his glass then sat there with both elbows on his knees and stared, unblinkingly and without expression, at the wrecked remains of his car.

Dunnet said: 'And only two months ago he'd never touched the hard stuff in his life. What are you going to do, James?'

'Now?' MacAlpine smiled faintly. 'I'm going to see Mary. I think by this time they might let me in to see her.' He glanced briefly, his face seemingly impassive, around the pits, at Harlow lifting his glass again, at the red-haired Rafferty twins looking almost as unhappy as Dunnet, and at Jacobson, Tracchia and Rory wearing uniform scowls and directing them in uniform directions, sighed for the last time, turned and walked heavily away.

Mary MacAlpine was twenty-two years old, pale complexioned despite the many hours she spent in the sun, with big brown eyes, gleamingly brushed black hair as dark as night and the most bewitching smile that ever graced a Grand Prix racing track: she did not intend that the smile should be bewitching, she just couldn't help it. Everyone in the team, even the taciturn and terrible-tempered Jacobson, was in love with her in one way or another, not to mention a quite remarkable number of other people who were not in the team: this Mary recognized and accepted with commendable aplomb, although without either amusement or condescension: condescension was quite alien to her nature. In any event, she viewed the regard that others had for her as only the natural reciprocal of the regard she had for them: despite her quick no-nonsense mind, Mary MacAlpine was in many ways still very young.

Lying in bed in that spotless, soullessly antiseptic hospital room that night, Mary MacAlpine looked younger than ever. She also looked, as she unquestionably was, very ill. The natural paleness had turned to pallor and the big brown eyes which she opened only briefly and reluctantly, were dulled with pain. This same pain was reflected in MacAlpine's eyes as he looked down at his daughter, at the heavily splinted and bandaged left leg lying on top of the sheet. MacAlpine stooped and kissed his daughter on the forehead.

He said: 'Sleep well, darling. Good night.'

She tried to smile. 'With all the pills they've given me? Yes, I think I will. And Daddy.'

'Darling?'

'It wasn't Johnny's fault. I know it wasn't. It was his car. I know it was.'

'We're finding that out. Jacobson is taking the car down.'

'You'll see. Will you ask Johnny to come and see me?'

'Not tonight, darling. I'm afraid he's not too well.'

'He – he hasn't been – '

'No, no. Shock.' MacAlpine smiled, 'He's been fed the same pills as yourself.'

'Johnny Harlow? In shock? I don't believe it. Three near-fatal crashes and he never once – '

'He saw you, my darling.' He squeezed her hand. 'I'll be around later tonight.'

MacAlpine left the room and walked down to the reception area. A doctor was speaking to the nurse at the desk. He had grey hair, tired eyes and the face of an aristocrat. MacAlpine said: 'Are you the person who is looking after my daughter?'

'Mr MacAlpine? Yes, I am. Dr Chollet.'

'She seems very ill.'

'No, Mr MacAlpine. No problem. She is just under heavy sedation. For the pain, you understand.'

'I see. How long will she be – '

'Two weeks. Perhaps three. No more.'

'One question, Dr Chollet. Why is her leg not in traction?'

'It would seem, Mr MacAlpine, that you are not a man who is afraid of the truth.'

'Why is her leg not in traction?'

'Traction is for broken bones, Mr MacAlpine. Your daughter's left ankle bone, I'm afraid, is not just broken, it is – how would you say it in English? – pulverized, yes I think that is the word, pulverized beyond any hope of remedial surgery.

What's left of the bone will have to be fused together.'

'Meaning that she can never bend her ankle again?' Chollet inclined his head. 'A permanent limp? For life?'

'You can have a second opinion, Mr MacAlpine. The best orthopaedic specialist in Paris. You are entitled – '

'No. That will not be necessary. The truth is obvious, Dr Chollet. One accepts the obvious.'

'I am deeply sorry, Mr MacAlpine. She is a lovely child. But I am only a surgeon. Miracles? No. No miracles.'

'Thank you, Doctor. You are most kind. I'll be back in about say – two hours?'

'Please not. She will be asleep for at least twelve hours. Perhaps sixteen.'

MacAlpine nodded his head in acceptance and left.

Dunnet pushed away his plate with his untouched meal, looked at MacAlpine's plate, similarly untouched, then at the brooding MacAlpine.

He said: 'I don't think either of us, James, is as tough as we thought we were.'

'Age, Alexis. It overtakes us all.'

'Yes. And at very high speed, it would seem.' Dunnet pulled his plate towards him, regarded it sorrowfully then pushed it away again.

'Well, I suppose it's a damn sight better than amputation.'

'There's that. There's that.' MacAlpine pushed back his chair. 'A walk, I think, Alexis.'

'For the appetite? It won't work. Not with me.'

'Nor with me. I just thought it might be interesting to see if Jacobson has turned up anything.'

The garage was very long, low, heavily skylighted, brilliantiy lit with hanging spotlights and, for a garage, was remarkably clean and tidy. Jacobson was at the inner end, stooped over Harlow's wrecked Coronado, when the metal door screeched open. He straightened, acknowledged the presence of MacAlpine and Dunnet with a wave of his hand, then returned to his examination of the car.

Dunnet closed the door and said quietly: 'Where are the other mechanics?'

MacAlpine said: You should know by this time. Jacobson always works alone on a crash job. A very low opinion of other mechanics, has Jacobson. Says they either overlook evidence or destroy it by clumsiness.'

The two men advanced and watched in silence as Jacobson tightened a connection in the hydraulic brake line. They were not alone in watching him. Directly above them, through an open skylight, the powerful lamps in the garage reflected on something metallic. The metallic object was a hand-held eight millimetre camera and the hands that held them were very steady indeed. They were the hands of Johnny Harlow. His face was as impassive as his hands were motionless, intent and still and totally watchful. He was also totally sober.

MacAlpine said: 'Well?'

Jacobson straightened and tenderly massaged an obviously aching back.

'Nothing. Just nothing. Suspension, brakes, engine, transmission, tyres, steering – all OK.'

'But the steering – '

'Sheared. Impact fracture. Couldn't be anything else. It was still working when he pulled out in front of Jethou. You can't tell me that the steering suddenly went in that one second of time, Mr MacAlpine. Coincidence is coincidence, but that would be just a bit too much.'

Dunnet said: 'So we're still in the dark?'

'It's broad daylight where I stand. The oldest reason in the business. Driver error.'

'Driver error.' Dunnet shook his head. 'Johnny Harlow never made a driver error in his life.'

Jacobson smiled, his eyes cold. 'I'd like to have the opinion of Jethou's ghost on that one.'

MacAlpine said: 'This hardly helps. Come on. Hotel. You haven't even eaten yet, Jacobson.' He looked at Dunnet. 'A night-cap in the bar, I think, then a look-in on Johnny.'

Jacobson said: 'You'll be wasting your time, sir. He'll be paralytic.'

MacAlpine looked at Jacobson consideringly, then said very slowly and after a long pause: 'He's still world champion. He's still Coronado's number one.'

'So that's the way of it, is it?'

'You want it some other way?'

Jacobson crossed to a sink, began to wash his hands. Without turning he said: 'You're the boss, Mr MacAlpine.'

MacAlpine made no reply. When Jacobson had dried his hands the three men left the garage in silence, closing the heavy metal door behind them.

Only the top half of Harlow's head and supporting hands were visible as he clung to the ridge-pole of the garage's V-roof and watched the three men walk up the brightly lit main street. As soon as they had turned a corner and disappeared from sight, he slid gingerly down towards the opened skylight, lowered himself through the opening and felt with his feet until he found a metal cross-beam. He released his grip on the skylight sill, balanced precariously on the beam, brought out a small flashlight from an inner pocket – Jacobson had switched off all the lights before leaving – and directed it downwards. The concrete floor was about nine feet below him.

Harlow stooped, reached for the beam with his hands, slid down over it, hung at the full stretch of his hand, then released his grip. He landed lightly and easily, headed for the door, switched on all the lights then went directly to the Coronado. He was carrying not one but two strap-hung cameras, his eight millimetre cine and a very compact still camera with flashlight attachment.

He found an oily cloth and used it to rub clean part of the right suspension, a fuel line, the steering linkage and one of the carburettors in the engine compartment. Each of these areas he flash-photographed several times with the still camera. He retrieved the cloth, coated it with a mixture of oil and dirt from the floor, swiftly smeared the parts he had photographed and threw the cloth into a metal bin provided for that purpose.

He crossed to the door and tugged on the handle, but to no avail. The door had been locked from the outside and its heavy construction precluded any thought or attempt to force it: and Harlow's last thought was to leave any trace of his passing. He looked quickly around the garage.

On his left hand side was a light wooden ladder suspended from two right-angle wall brackets – a ladder almost certainly reserved for the cleaning of the very considerable skylight area. Below it, and to one side, lay, in a corner, the untidy coil of a towrope.

Harlow moved to the corner, picked up the rope, lifted the ladder off its brackets, looped the rope round the top rung and placed the ladder against the metal cross-beam. He returned to the door and switched off the lights. Using his flashlight, he climbed up the ladder and straddled the beam. Grasping the ladder while still maintaining his grip on the rope, he manœuvred the former until the lower end hooked on to one of the right-angle wall brackets. Using the looped rope, he lowered the other end of the ladder until, not without some difficulty, he managed to drop it into the other bracket. He released one end of the rope, pulled it clear of the ladder, coiled it up and threw it into the corner where it had been previously lying. Then, swaying dangerously, he managed to bring himself upright on the beam, thrust himself head and shoulders through the opened skylight, hauled himself up and disappeared into the night above.

MacAlpine and Dunnet were seated alone at a table in an otherwise deserted lounge bar. They were seated in silence as a waiter brought them two scotches. MacAlpine raised his glass and smiled without humour.

'When you come to the end of a perfect day. God, I'm tired.'

'So you're committed, James. So Harlow goes on.'

'Thanks to Jacobson. Didn't leave me much option, did he?'

Harlow, running along the brightly lit main street, stopped abruptly. The street was almost entirely deserted except for two tall men approaching his way. Harlow hesitated, looked around swiftly, then pressed into a deeply recessed shop entrance. He stood there immobile as the two men passed by: they were Nicolo Tracchia, Harlow's team-mate, and Willi Neubauer, engrossed in low-voiced and clearly very earnest conversation. Neither of them saw Harlow. They passed by. Harlow emerged from the recessed doorway, looked cautiously both ways, waited until the retreating backs of Tracchia and Neubauer had turned a corner, then broke into a run again.

MacAlpine and Dunnet drained their glasses. MacAlpine looked questioningly at Dunnet. Dunnet said: 'Well, I suppose we've got to face it some time.'

MacAlpine said: 'I suppose.' Both men rose, nodded to the barman, and left.

Harlow, now moving at no more than a fast walk, crossed the street in the direction of a neon-signed hotel. Instead of using the main entrance, he went down a side alleyway, turned to his right and started to climb a fire-escape two steps at a time. His steps were as sure-footed as a mountain goat, his balance immaculate, his face registering no emotion. Only his eyes registered any expression. They were clear and still but possessed an element of clear-eyed and concentrated calculation. It was the face of a dedicated man who knew completely what he was about.

MacAlpine and Dunnet were outside a door, numbered 412. MacAlpine's face registered a peculiar mixture of anger and concern. Dunnet's face, oddly, showed only unconcern. It could have been tight-lipped unconcern, but then Dunnet was habitually a tight-lipped man. MacAlpine hammered loudly on the door. The hammering brought no reaction. MacAlpine glanced furiously at his bruising knuckles, glanced at Dunnet and started a renewed assault on the door. Dunnet had no comment to make, either vocally or facially.

Harlow reached a platform on the fourth-floor fire-eseape. He swung over the guard-railing, took a long step towards a nearby open window, negotiated the crossing safely and passed inside. The room was small. A suitcase lay on the floor, its contents spilled out in considerable disarray. On the bedside table stood a low-wattage lamp, which gave the only weak illumination in the room, and a half empty bottle of whisky. Harlow closed and locked the window to the accompaniment of a violent tattoo of knocks on the door. MacAlpine's outraged voice was very loud and clear.

'Open up! Johnny! Open up or I'll break the bloody door in.'

Harlow pushed both cameras under the bed. He tore off his black leather jacket and black roll-neck pull-over and thrust them both after the cameras. He then took a quick swill of whisky, split a little in the palm of his hand and rubbed it over his face.

The door burst open to show MacAlpine's outstretched right leg, the heel of which he'd obviously used against the lock. Both MacAlpine and Dunnet entered, then stood still. Harlow, clad only in shirt and trousers and still wearing his shoes, was stretched out in bed, apparently in an almost coma-like condition. His arm dangled over the side of the bed, his right hand clutching the neck of the whisky bottle. MacAlpine, grim-faced and almost incredulous, approached the bed, bent over Harlow, sniffed in disgust and removed the bottle from Harlow's nerveless hand. He looked at Dunnet, who returned his expressionless glance.

MacAlpine said: 'The greatest driver in the world.'

'Please James. You said it yourself. It happens to all of them. Remember? Sooner or later, it happens to them all.'

'But Johnny Harlow?'

'Even to Johnny Harlow.'

MacAlpine nodded. Both men turned and left the room, closing the broken door behind them. Harlow opened his eyes, rubbed his chin thoughtfully. His hand stopped moving and he sniffed his palm. He wrinkled his nose in distaste.

CHAPTER THREE

As the crowded weeks after the Clermont-Ferrand race rushed by there appeared to be little change in Johnny Harlow. Always a remote, withdrawn and lonely figure, remote and withdrawn he still remained, except that he was now more lonely than ever. In his great days, at the peak of his powers and the height of his fame, he had been a man relaxed to the point of abnormality, his inner self under iron control: and so, in his quietness, he seemed to be now, as aloofly remote and detached as ever, those remarkable eyes – remarkable in the quality of their phenomenal eyesight, not in appearance – as clear and calm and unblinking as ever and the aquiline face quite devoid of expression.

The hands were still now, hands that bespoke a man at peace with himself, but it would seem likely that the hands belied and did not bespeak for it seemed equally that he was not at peace with himself and never would be again for to say that Johnny Harlow's fortunes steadily declined from that day he had killed Jethou and crippled Mary one would be guilty of a sad misuse of the English language. They hadn't declined, they had collapsed with what must have been for him – and most certainly for his great circle of friends, acquaintances and admirers – a complete and shattering finality.

Two weeks after the death of Jethou – and this before his own home British crowd who had come, almost to a man, to forgive him for the dreadful insults and accusations heaped upon him by the French press and to cheer their idol home to victory – he had suffered the indignity, not to say the humiliation, of running off the track in the very first lap. He had caused no damage either to himself or any spectator but his Coronado was a total write-off. As both front tyres had burst it was assumed that at least one of them had gone before the car had left the track: there could not, it was agreed, have been any other explanation for Harlow's abrupt departure into the wilderness. This agreement was not quite universal. Jacobson, predictably, had privately expressed his opinion that the accepted explanation was a very charitable assumption indeed. Jacobson was becoming very attached to the phrase 'driver error'.

Two weeks after that, at the German Grand Prix – probably the most difficult circuit in Europe but one of which Harlow was an acknowledged master – the air of gloom and despondency that hung like a thundercloud over the Coronado pits was almost palpable enough, almost visible enough to take hold of and push to one side – were it not for the fact that this particular cloud was immovable. The race was over and the last of the Grand Prix cars had vanished to complete the final circuit of the track before coming into their pits.

MacAlpine, looking both despondent and bitter, glanced at Dunnet, who lowered his eyes, bit his lower lip and shook his head. MacAlpine looked away and lost himself in his own private thoughts. Mary sat on a canvas chair close beside them. Her left leg was still in heavy plaster and crutches were propped up against her chair. She held a lap-time note-pad in one hand, a stop watch and pencil in the other. She was gnawing a pencil and her pale face held the expression of one who was pretty close to tears. Behind her stood Jacobson, his two mechanics, and Rory. Jacobson's face, if his habitual saturnine expression were excepted, was quite without expression. His mechanics, the red-haired Rafferty twins, wore, as usual, identical expressions, in this case a mixture of resignation and despair. Rory's face registered nothing but a cold contempt.

Rory said: 'Eleventh out of twelve finishers! Boy, what a driver. Our world champion – doing his lap of honour, I suppose.'

Jacobson looked at him speculatively.

'A month ago he was your idol, Rory.'

Rory looked across at his sister. She was still gnawing her pencil, the shoulders were drooped and the tears in her eyes were now unmistakable. Rory looked back at Jacobson and said: 'That was a month ago.'

A lime-green Coronado swept into the pits, braked and stopped, its crackling exhaust fading away into silence. Nicolo Tracchia removed his helmet, produced a large silk handkerchief, wiped his matinée-idol face and started to remove his gloves. He looked, and with reason, particularly pleased with himself, for he had just finished second and that by only a car's length. MacAlpine crossed to him and patted the still-seated Tracchia on the back.

'A magnificent race, Nikki. Your best ever – and on this brute of a course. Your third second place in five times out.' He smiled. 'You know, I'm beginning to think that we may make a driver of you yet.'

Tracchia grinned hugely and climbed from the car.

'Watch me next time out. So far, Nicolo Tracchia hasn't really been trying, just trying to improve the performance of those machines our chief mechanic ruins for us between races.' He smiled at Jacobson, who grinned back: despite the marked differences in the natures and interests, there was a close affinity between the two men. 'Now, when it comes to the Austrian Grand Prix in a couple of weeks – well, I'm sure you can afford a couple of bottles of champagne.'

MacAlpine smiled again and it was clear that though the smile did not come easily its reluctance was not directed against Tracchia. In the space of one brief month MacAlpine, even though he still couldn't conceivably be called a thin person, had noticeably lost weight in both body and face, the already trenched lines in the latter seemed to have deepened and it was possible even to imagine an increase in the silver on that magnificent head of hair. It was difficult to imagine that even the precipitous fall from grace of his superstar could have been responsible for so dramatic a change but it was equally difficult to imagine that there could have been any other reason. MacAlpine said:

'Overlooking the fact, aren't we, that there'll be a real live Austrian at the Austrian Grand Prix. Chap called Willi Neubauer. You *have* heard of him?'

Tracchia was unperturbed. 'Austrian our Willi may be, but the Austrian Grand Prix is not his circuit. He's never come in better than fourth. I've been second in the last two years.' He glanced away as another Coronado entered the pits then looked back at MacAlpine. 'And you know who came in first both times.'

'Yes, I know.' MacAlpine turned away heavily and approached the other car as Harlow got out, removed his helmet, looked at his car and shook his head. When MacAlpine spoke there was no bitterness or anger or accusation in either voice or face, just a faint resignation and despair.

'Well, Johnny, you can't win them all.'

Harlow said: 'Not with this car I can't.'

'Meaning?'

'Loss of power in the higher revs.'

Jacobson had approached and his face was still without expression as he heard Harlow's explanation. He said: 'From the start?'

'No. Nothing to do with you, Jake, I know that. It was bloody funny. Kept coming and going. At least a dozen times I got full power back. But never for long.' He turned away and moodily examined his car again. Jacobson glanced at MacAlpine, who gave him an all but imperceptible nod.

By dusk that evening the race-track was deserted, the last of the crowds and officials gone. MacAlpine, a lonely and brooding figure, his hands thrust deeply in the pockets of his tan gaberdine suit, stood at the entrance of the Coronado pits. He wasn't, however, quite as alone as he might justifiably have imagined. In the neighbouring Cagliari pits a figure clad in a dark roll-neck pullover and dark leather jacket stood hidden in a shadowed corner. Johnny Harlow had a remarkable capacity for maintaining an absolute stillness and that capacity he was employing to the full at that moment. But apart from those two figures the entire track seemed quite empty of life.

But not of sound. There came the deepening clamour of the sound of a Grand Prix engine and a Coronado, lights on, appeared from the distance, changed down through the gears, slowed right down as it passed the Cagliari pits and came to a halt outside the entrance to the Coronado pits. Jacobson climbed out and removed his helmet.

MacAlpine said: 'Well?'

'Damn all the matter with the car.' His tone was neutral but his eyes were hard. 'Went like a bird. Our Johnny certainly knows how to use his imagination. We've got something more than just driver error here, Mr MacAlpine.'

MacAlpine hesitated. The fact that Jacobson had made a perfect lap circuit was no proof of anything one way or another. In the nature of things he would have been unable to drive the Coronado at anything like the speed Harlow had done. Again, the fault may have occurred only when the engine had heated to its maximum and it was unlikely that Jacobson could have reached that in a single lap: finally, those highly-bred racing engines, which could cost up to eight thousand pounds, were extraordinarily fickle creatures and quite capable of developing and clearing up their own faults without the hand of man going anywhere near them. Jacobson, inevitably, regarded MacAlpine's silence as either doubt or outright agreement. He said: 'Maybe you're coming round to my way of thinking, Mr MacAlpine?'

MacAlpine didn't say whether he was or he wasn't. He said instead: 'Just leave the car where she is. We'll send Henry and the two boys down with the transporter to pick it up. Come along.

Dinner. I think we've earned it. And a drink. I think we've earned that, too. In fact I don't think I've ever earned so many drinks as I have in the past four weeks.'

'I wouldn't disagree with you on that, Mr MacAlpine.'

MacAlpine's blue Aston Martin lay parked in the rear of the pits. Both men climbed in and drove off down the track.

Harlow watched the car depart. If he had been disturbed by the conclusions Jacobson had arrived at or MacAlpine's apparent acceptance of them no signs of any such anxiety were reflected in his untroubled face. He waited until the car had disappeared into the gathering darkness, looked round carefully to make sure that he was entirely alone and unobserved, then moved into the back of the Cagliari pits. There he opened a canvas bag he was carrying, produced a flat-based lamp-light with a large swivelling head, a hammer, cold chisel and screwdriver and set them on top of the nearest crate. He pressed the switch on the handle of the lamp-light and a powerful white beam illuminated the back of the Cagliari pits. A flick on the lever on the base of the swivelling head and the white dazzle was at once replaced by a red muted glow. Harlow took hammer and chisel in hand and set resolutely to work.

Most of the crates and boxes did not, in fact, have to be forced for the esoteric collection of engine and chassis spares inside them could not conceivably have been of any interest to any passing thief: he almost certainly wouldn't have known what to look for and, in the remote event of his so knowing, he would quite certainly have been unable to dispose of them. The few crates that Harlow did have to open he did so carefully, gently and with the minimum of noise.

Harlow spent the minimum of time on his examination, presumably because delay always increased the danger of discovery. He also appeared to know exactly what he was looking for. The contents of some boxes were disposed of with only the most cursory of glances: even the largest of the crates merited no more than a minute's inspection. Within half an hour after beginning the operation he had begun to close all the crates and boxes up again. Those he had been compelled to force open he closed with a cloth-headed hammer to reduce noise to a minimum and leave the least perceptible traces of his passing. When he was finished, he returned his torch and tools to the canvas bag, emerged from the Cagliari pits and walked away into the near darkness. If he was disappointed with the results of his investigation he did not show it: but, then, Harlow rarely showed any emotion.

Fourteen days later Nicolo Tracchia achieved what he promised MacAlpine he would achieve – the ambition of his life. He won the Austrian Grand Prix. Harlow, by now predictably, won nothing. Worse, not only did he not finish the race, he hardly even began it, achieving only four more laps than he had in England – and there he had crashed on the first lap.

He had begun well enough By any standards, even his own, he had made a brilliantly successful start and was leading the field by a clear margin after the end of the fifth lap. Next time round he pulled his Coronado into the pits. As he stepped out of his car he seemed normal enough with no trace of undue anxiety and nothing even closely resembling a cold sweat. But he had his hands thrust deeply into his overall pockets and his fists were tightly balled: this way you can't tell whether a man's hands are shaking or not. He removed one hand long enough to make a dismissive gesture towards all the pit crew – with the exception of the still chair-borne Mary – who came hurrying towards him.

'No panic.' He shook his head. 'And no hurry. Fourth gear's gone.' He stood looking out moodily over the track. MacAlpine stared at him closely then looked at Dunnet who nodded without even appearing to have seen the glance that MacAlpine had directed at him. Dunnet was staring at the clenched hands inside Harlow's pockets.

MacAlpine said: 'We'll pull Nikki in. You can have his car.'

Harlow didn't answer immediately. There came the sound of an approaching racing engine and Harlow nodded towards the track. The others followed his line of sight. A lime-green Coronado flashed by but still Harlow stared out over the track. At least another fifteen seconds elapsed before the next car, Neubauer's royal blue Cagliari came by. Harlow turned and looked at MacAlpine. Harlow's normally impassive face had come as near as it was possible for it to register a degree of incredulity.

'Pull him in? Good God, Mac, are you mad? Nikki's got fifteen clear seconds now that I'm out. There's no way he can lose. Our Signor Tracchia would never forgive me – or you – if you were to pull him in now. It'll be his first Grand Prix – and the one he most wanted to win.'

Harlow turned and walked away as if the matter was settled. Both Mary and Rory watched him go, the former with dull misery in her eyes, the latter with a mixture of triumph and contempt at which he was at no pains at all to conceal. MacAlpine hesitated, made as if to speak, then he too turned and walked away, although in a different direction. Dunnet accompanied him. The two men halted in a corner of the pits.

MacAlpine said: 'Well?'

Dunnet said: 'Well what, James?'

'Please. I don't deserve that from you.'

'You mean, did I see what you saw? His hands?'

'He's got the shakes again.' MacAlpine made a long pause then sighed and shook his head. 'I keep on saying it. It happens to them all. No matter how cool or brave or brilliant – hell, I've said it all before. And when a man has icy calm and iron control like Johnny – well, when the break comes it's liable to be a pretty drastic one.'

'And when does the break come?'

'Pretty soon, I think. I'll give him one more Grand Prix. Do you know what he's going to do now? Later tonight, rather – he's become very crafty about it.'

'I don't think I want to know.'

'He's going to hit the bottle.'

A voice with a very powerful Glasgow accent said: 'The word is that he already has.'

Both MacAlpine and Dunnet turned slowly round. Coming out of the shadows of the hut behind was a small man with an incredibly wizened face, whose straggling white moustache contrasted oddly with his monk's tonsure. Even odder was the long, thin and remarkably bent black cigar protruding from one corner of his virtually toothless mouth. His name was Henry, he was the transporter's old driver – long long past retiring age – and the cigar was his trademark. It was said that he occasionally ate with the cigar in his mouth.

MacAlpine said without inflection: 'Eavesdropping, eh?'

'Eavesdropping! 'It was difficult to say whether Henry's tone and expression reflected indignation or incredulity but in either event they were on an Olympian scale. 'You know very well that I would never eavesdrop, Mr MacAlpine. I was just listening. There's a difference.'

'What did you say just now?'

'I know you heard what I said.' Henry was still splendidly unperturbed. 'You know that he's driving like a madman and that all the other drivers are getting terrified of him. In fact, they *are* terrified of him. He shouldn't be allowed on a racetrack again. The man's shot, you can see that. And in Glasgow, when we say that a man's shot, we mean – '

Dunnet said: 'We know what you mean. I thought you were a friend of his, Henry?'

'Aye, I'm all that. Finest gentleman I've ever known, begging the pardon of you two gentlemen. It's because I'm his friend that I don't want him killed – or had up for manslaughter.'

MacAlpine said without animosity: 'You stick to your job of running the transporter, Henry: I'll stick to mine of running the Coronado team.'

Henry nodded and turned away, gravity in his face and a certain carefully controlled degree of outrage in his walk as if to say he'd done his duty, delivered his witch's warning and if that warning were not acted upon the consequences weren't going to be his, Henry's, fault. MacAlpine, his face equally grave, rubbed his cheek thoughtfully and said: 'He could be right at that. In fact, I have every reason for thinking he is.'

'Is what, James?'

'On the skids. On the rocks. Shot, as Henry would say.'

'Shot by whom? By what?'

'Chap called Bacchus, Alexis. The chap that prefers using booze to bullets.'

'You have evidence of this?'

'Not so much evidence of his drinking as lack of evidence of his not drinking. Which can be just as damning.'

'Sorry, don't follow. Can it be that you have been holding out on me, James?'

MacAlpine nodded and told briefly of his duplicity in the line of duty. It was just after the day that Jethou had died and Harlow had shown his lack of expertise both in pouring and drinking brandy that MacAlpine had first suspected that Harlow had forgone his lifelong abstention from alcohol. There had been, of course, no spectacular drinking bouts, for those would have been automatically responsible for having him banned from the race-tracks of the world: a genius for avoiding company, he just went about it quietly, steadily, persistently and above all secretly, for Harlow always drank alone, almost invariably in out of the way places, usually quite remote, where he stood little or no chance of being discovered. This MacAlpine knew for he had hired what was practically a full-time investigator to follow him but Harlow was either extremely lucky or, aware of what was going on – he was a man of quite remarkable intelligence and must have suspected the possibility of his being followed – extremely astute and skilled in his avoidance of surveillance, for he had been tracked down only three times to sources of supply, small *Weinstuben* lost in the forests near the Hocken-heim and Nurburgring circuits. Even on those occasions he had been observed to be sipping, delicately and with what appeared to be commendable restraint, a small glass of hock which was hardly sufficient to blunt even the highly-tuned faculties and reactions of a Formula One driver: what made this elusiveness all the more remarkable was that Harlow drove everywhere in his flame-red Ferrari, the most conspicuous car on the roads of Europe. But that he went to such extraordinary – and extraordinarily successful – lengths to escape surveillance was, for MacAlpine, all the circumstantial evidence he required that Harlow's frequent, mysterious and unexplained absences coincided with Harlow's frequent and solitary drinking bouts. MacAlpine finished by saying that a later and more sinister note had crept in: there was now daily and incontrovertible evidence that Harlow had developed a powerful affinity for scotch.

Dunnet was silent until he saw that MacAlpine apparently had no intention of adding to what he had said. 'Evidence?' he said, 'What kind of evidence?'

'Olfactory evidence.'

Dunnet paused briefly then said: 'I've never smelt anything.'

MacAlpine said kindly: 'That, Alexis, is because you are not capable of smelling anything. You can't smell oil, you can't smell fuel, you can't smell burning tyres. How do you expect to be able to smell scotch?'

Dunnet inclined his head in acknowledgment. He said: 'Have you smelt anything?'

MacAlpine shook his head.

'Well, then.'

MacAlpine said: 'He avoids me like the plague nowadays – and you know how close Johnny and myself used to be. Whenever he does get close to me he smells powerfully of menthol throat tablets. Doesn't that say something to you?'

'Come off it, James. That's no evidence.'

'Perhaps not. But Tracchia, Jacobson and Rory swear to it.'

'Oh, brother, are they unbiased witnesses. If Johnny is forced to step down who's going to be Coronado's number one driver with a good chance of being the next champion? Who but our Nikki. Jacobson and Johnny have never been on good terms and now the relationship is going from bad to worse: Jacobson doesn't like having his cars smashed up and what he likes even less is Harlow's contention that the smashes have nothing to do with him which bring;s into question Jacobson's ability to prepare a car thoroughly. As for Rory, well, frankly, he hates Johnny Harlow's guts: partly because of what Johnny did to Mary, partly because she's never allowed the accident to make the slightest difference in her attitude towards him. I'm afraid, James, that your daughter is the only person left on the team who is still totally devoted to Johnny Harlow.'

'Yes, I know.' MacAlpine was momentarily silent then said dully: 'Mary was the first person to tell me.'

'Oh, Jesus!' Dunnet looked miserably out on the track and without looking at MacAlpine said: 'You've no option now. You have to fire him. For preference, today.'

'You're forgetting, Alexis, that you've just learnt this while I've known it for some time. My mind has been made up. One more Grand Prix.'

The parking lot, in the fading light, looked like the last resting place of the behemoths of a bygone age. The huge transporters that carried the racing cars, spare parts and portable workshops around Europe, parked, as they were, in a totally haphazard fashion, loomed menacingly out of the gloom. They were completely devoid of life as evinced by the fact that no light showed from any of them. The car park itself was equally deserted except for a figure that had just appeared from out of the gathering dusk and passed through the entrance to the transporter parking lot.

Johnny Harlow made no apparent attempt to conceal his presence from any chance observer, if any such there had been. Swinging his little canvas bag he made his way diagonally across the parking lot until he brought up at one of the huge behemoths: written large on the side and back was the word FERRARI. He didn't even bother to try the door of the transporter but produced a bunch of curiously shaped keys and had the door open in a matter of a few seconds. He passed inside and closed and locked the door behind him. For five minutes he did nothing other than move from window to window on either side of the transporter checking patiently, continuously, to see if his unauthorized entrance had been observed. It was apparent that it had not been. Satisfied, Harlow withdrew the flash-lamp from the canvas bag, switched on the red beam, stooped over the nearest Ferrari racing car and began to examine it minutely.

There were about thirty people in the hotel lobby that evening. Among them were Mary MacAlpine and her brother, Henry and the two red-haired Rafferty twins. The sound level of the conversation was notably high: the hotel had been taken over for the weekend by several of the Grand Prix teams and the racing fraternity is not particularly renowned for its inhibitions. All of them, mainly drivers but with several mechanics, had discarded their workaday clothes and were suitably attired for their evening meal which was as yet an hour distant. Henry, especially, was exceptionally resplendent in a grey pin-striped suit with a red rose in his buttonhole. Even his moustache appeared to have been combed. Mary sat beside him with Rory a few feet away, reading a magazine, or at least appearing to do so. Mary sat silently, unsmiling, constantly gripping and twisting one of the walking sticks to which she had now graduated. Suddenly, she turned to Henry.

'Where *does* Johnny go each evening. We hardly ever see him after dinner nowadays.'

'Johnny?' Henry adjusted the flower in his button, hole. 'No idea, miss. Maybe he prefers his own company. Maybe he finds the food better elsewhere. Maybe anything.'

Rory still held the magazine before his face. Clearly however he was not reading for his eyes were very still. But, at the moment, his whole being was not in his eyes but in his ears.

Mary said: 'Maybe it's not just the food that he finds better elsewhere.'

'Girls, miss? Johnny Harlow's not interested in girls.' He leered at her in what he probably imagined to be a roguish fashion in keeping with the gentlemanly splendour of his evening wear. 'Except for a certain you-know-who.'

Don't be such a fool.' Mary MacAlpine was not always milk and roses. 'You know what I mean.'

'What *do* you mean, miss?'

'Don't be clever with me, Henry.'

Henry assumed the sad expression of the continuously misjudged.

'I'm not clever enough to be clever with anybody.'

Mary looked at him in cold speculation then abruptly turned away. Rory just as quickly averted his own head. He was looking very thoughtful indeed and the expression superimposed upon the thoughtfulness could hardly be described as pleasant.

Harlow, the hooded red light giving all the illumination he required, probed the depths of a box of spares. Suddenly, he half straightened, cocked his head as if to listen, switched off the torch, went to a side window and peered out. The evening darkness had deepened until it was now almost night, but a yellowish half-moon drifting behind scattered cloud gave just enough light to see by. Two men were heading across the transporter park, heading straight towards the Coronado unit, which was less than twenty feet from where Harlow stood watching. There was no difficulty at all in identifying them as MacAlpine and Jacobson. Harlow made his way to the Ferrari transporter's door, unlocked it and cautiously opened it just sufficiently to give him a view of the Coronado transporter's door. MacAlpine was just inserting his key in the lock. MacAlpine said:

'So there's no doubt then. Harlow wasn't imagining things. Fourth gear is stripped.'

'Completely.'

'So he may be in the clear after all?' There was a note almost of supplication in MacAlpine's voice.

'There's more than one way of stripping a gear.' Jacobson's tone offered very little in the way of encouragement.

'There's that, I suppose, there's that. Come on, let's have a look at this damned gear-box.'

Both men passed inside and lights came on. Harlow, unusually half-smiling, nodded slowly, closed and gently locked the door and resumed his search. He acted with the same circumspection as he had in the Cagliari pits, forcing open crates and boxes, when this was necessary, with the greatest of care so that they could be closed again to show the absolute minimum of offered violence. He operated with speed and intense concentration, pausing only once at the sound of a noise outside. He checked the source of the noise, saw MacAlpine and Jacobson descending the steps of the Coronado transporter and walk away acrossthe deserted compound. Harlow returned to his work.

CHAPTER FOUR

When Harlow finally returned to the hotel, the lobby, which also served as the bar, was crowded with hardly a seat left vacant and a group of at least a dozen men pressing in close against the bar. MacAlpine and Jacobson were sitting at a table with Dunnet. Mary, Henry and Rory were still sitting in the same seats. As Harlow closed the street door behind him, the dinner gong sounded – it was that kind of small country hotel, deliberately so styled, where everyone ate at the same time or not at all. It was a great convenience to management and staff though somewhat less so to the guests.

The guests were rising as Harlow made his way across the lobby towards the stairs. Nobody greeted him, few even bothered to look at him. MacAlpine, Jacobson and Dunnet ignored him entirely. Rory scowled at him in open contempt. Mary glanced briefly at him, bit her lip and quickly looked away again. Two months previously it would have taken Johnny Harlow five minutes to reach the foot of those stairs. That evening he made it in under ten seconds. If he was in any way dismayed by his reception he hid his concern well. His face was as impassive as that of a wooden Indian's.

Arrived in his bedroom, he washed cursorily, combed his hair, crossed to a cupboard, reached for a high shelf, brought down a bottle of scotch, went into the bathroom, sipped some of the scotch, swirled it round his mouth then grimaced and spat it out. He left the glass, with its still almost untouched contents, on the basin ledge, returned the bottle to the cupboard and made his way down to the dining-room.

He was the last arrival. A complete stranger entering would have been paid more attention than was accorded to him. Harlow was no longer the person to be seen with. The dining-room was pretty well filled but not to capacity. Most of the tables held four people, a handful held only two. Of the tables that held four people, only three had as few as three people at them. Of the tables for two, only Henry sat alone. Harlow's mouth quirked, so briefly, perhaps even involuntarily, that it could have been more imagined than seen, then, without hesitation, he crossed the dining-room and sat down at Henry's table.

Harlow said: 'May I, Henry?'

'Be my guest, Mr Harlow.' Henry was cordiality itself, and cordial he remained throughout the meal, talking at length on a wide variety of utterly inconsequential subjects which, try as he might, Harlow found of only minimal interest. Henry's intellectual reach was normally limited in its nature and Harlow found that it was only with considerable difficulty that he could keep up his conversational end against Henry's pedestrian platitudes. To make matters worse he had to listen to Henry's observations from a distance of about six inches, an aesthetic ordeal in itself, as at even a distance of several yards Henry could not, with all charity, have been called photogenic. But Henry appeared to have considered this close-range exchange of intimacies as essential and, in the circumstances, Harlow would have found it hard to disagree with him. The silence in the dining-room that evening was more in the nature of a cathedral hush, one that could not have been attributed to a beatific enjoyment of the food which was of a standard to earn for the Austrians the most astronomical odds against in the culinary stakes. It was plain to Harlow, as it was plain to all present, that the very fact of his being there had an almost totally inhibitory effect on normal conversation. Henry, consequently, considered it prudent to lower his voice to a graveyard whisper that could not be heard beyond the confines of their table which in turn necessitated this very personal face-to-face approach. Harlow felt but did not express his profound relief when the meal was over: Henry also suffered from a severe case of halitosis.

Harlow was among the last to rise. He drifted aimlessly into the now again crowded lobby. He stood there in apparent irresolution, quite ignored and glancing idly around. Mary he saw there, and Rory, while at the far end of the lobby MacAlpine was engaged with what appeared to be some form of desultory conversation with Henry.

MacAlpine said: 'Well?'

Henry was wearing his self-righteous expression. 'Smelled like a distillery, sir.'

MacAlpine smiled faintly. 'Coming from Glasgow, you should know something about those things. A good job. I owe you an apology, Henry.'

Henry inclined his head. 'Granted, Mr MacAlpine.'

Harlow averted his head from this tableau. He hadn't heard a word of the exchange but then he didn't have to hear it. Suddenly, like a man making up his mind, he headed for the street door. Mary saw him go, looked around to see if she was being observed, came to the apparent conclusion that she wasn't, gathered up her two sticks and limped after him. Rory, in his turn, waited for about ten seconds after his sister's departure then drifted aimlessly towards the door.

Five minutes later Harlow entered a café and took a seat at an empty table where he could keep an eye on the entrance. A pretty young waitress approached, opened her eyes and then smiled charmingly. There were few young people of either sex in Europe who did not recognize Harlow on sight.

Harlow smiled back. 'Tonic and water, please.'

The eyes opened even wider. 'I beg your pardon, sir.'

'Tonic and water.'

The waitress, whose opinion of world champion drivers had clearly suffered a sudden revision, brought the drink. He sipped it occasionally, keeping an eye on the entrance door, then frowned as the door opened and Mary, clearly in a very apprehensive mood, entered the café. She saw Harlow at once, limped across the room and sat down at the table.

She said: 'Hallo, Johnny,' in the voice of one who was far from sure of her reception.

'I must say I'd expected someone else.'

'You what?'

'Someone else,'

'I don't understand. Who – '

'No matter.' Harlow's tone was as brusque as his words. 'Who sent you here to spy on me?'

'Spy on you? Spy on you?' She stared at him, the expression on her face one of lack of understanding rather than incredulity. 'What on earth can you mean?'

Harlow remained implacable. 'Surely you know what the word "spy" means?'

'Oh, Johnny!' The hurt in the big brown eyes was as unmistakable as that in the voice. 'You know I'd never spy on you.'

Harlow relented, but only marginally. 'Then why are you here?'

'Aren't you pleased just to see me?'

'That's neither here nor there. What are you doing in this café?'

'I was – I was just passing by and – '

'And you saw me and came in.' Abruptly he pushed back his chain and rose. 'Wait here.'

Harlow went to the front door, glanced at it briefly and opened it, stepping just outside. He turned and looked for several seconds back up the way he had come, then turned round and looked down the street. But his interest lay in neither direction, but in a doorway directly across the street. A figure stood there, pushed back deeply into the recess. Without appearing to have noticed him, Harlow re-entered the café, closed the door behind him and returned to his seat.

He said: 'Aren't you lucky to have those X-ray eyes. Frosted glass all the way and yet you see me sitting here.'

'All right, Johnny.' She sounded very weary. 'I followed you. I'm worried. I'm dreadfully worried.'

'Aren't we all now and again. You should see me out on those race-tracks at times.' He paused, then added with apparent inconsequence: 'Was Rory still in the hotel when you left?'

She blinked her puzzlement. 'Yes. Yes he was. I saw him. Just as I was leaving.'

'Could he have seen you?'

'That's a funny question.'

'I'm a funny fellow. Ask anyone around the racetracks. Could he have seen you?'

'Well, yes, I suppose he could. Why – why all this concern about Rory?'

'I wouldn't like the poor little lad to be abroad in the streets at night and maybe catch a chill. Or maybe even get mugged.' Harlow paused consideringly. 'There's a thought, now.'

'Oh, stop it, Johnny! Stop it! I know, well I know he can't stand the sight of you, won't even speak to you ever since – ever since – '

'Ever since I crippled you.'

'Oh, dear God!' The distress in the face was very real. 'He's my brother, Johnny, but he's not me. Can I help it if – look, whatever his grudge, can't you forget it? You're the kindest man in the world, Johnny Harlow – '

'Kindness doesn't pay, Mary.'

'You still are. I know you are. Can't you forget it? Can't you forgive him? You're big enough, much more than big enough. Besides, he's only a boy. You're a man. What danger is he to you? What harm can he do you?'

'You should see what harm a dangerous nine-year-old can do in Vietnam when he has a rifle in his hands.'

She pushed her chair back. The tonelessness in her voice belied the tears in her eyes. She said: 'Please forgive me. I shouldn't have bothered you. Good night, Johnny.'

He laid a gentle hand on her wrist and she made no move to withdraw it, merely sat waiting there with a numbed despair on her face. He said: 'Don't go. I just wanted to make sure of something.'

'What?'

'Oddly, it doesn't matter any more. Let's forget about Rory. Let's talk of you.' He called to the waitress. 'Same again, please.'

Mary looked at the freshly filled glass. She said: 'What's that? Gin? Vodka?'

'Tonic and water.'

'Oh, Johnny!'

'Will you kindly stop "Oh, Johnnying me".' It was impossible to tell whether the irritation in his voice was genuine or not. 'Now then. You say you are worried – as if you have to tell anyone that, far less me. Let me guess at your worries, Mary. I would say that there are five of them, Rory, yourself, your father, your mother and me.' She made as if to speak but he waved her to silence. 'You can forget about Rory and his antagonism to me. A month from now and he'll think it was all a bad dream. Then yourself – and don't deny you are worried about our, shall we say, relationship: those things tend to mend but they take time. Then there's your father and mother and, well, me again. I'm about right?'

'You haven't talked to me like this for a long long time.'

'Does that mean I'm about right?'

She nodded without speaking.

'Your father. I know he's not looking well, that he's lost weight. I suggest that he's worried about your mother and me, very much in that order.'

'My mother,' she whispered. 'How did you know about that? *Nobody* knows about that except Daddy and me.'

'I suspect Alexis Dunnet may know about it, they're very close friends, but I can't be sure. But your father told me, over two months ago. He trusted me, I know, in the days when we were still on speaking terms.'

'Please, Johnny.'

'Well, I suppose that's better than "Oh, Johnny". In spite of all that's passed, I believe he still does. Please don't tell him that I told you because I said I'd tell no one. Promise?'

'Promise.'

'Your father hasn't been very communicative in the past two months. Understandably. And I hardly felt I was in a position to ask him questions. No progress, no trace of her, no message since she left your Marseilles home three months ago?'

'Nothing, nothing.' If she'd been the type to wring her hands she'd have done just that. 'And she used to phone every day she wasn't with us, write every week and now we – '

'And your father has tried everything?'

'Daddy's a millionaire. Don't *you* think he would have tried everything?'

'I should have thought so. So. You're worried. What can I do?'

Mary briefly drummed her fingers on the table and looked up at him. Her eyes were masked in tears. She said: 'You could remove his other main worry.'

'Me?'

Mary nodded.

At that precise moment MacAlpine was very actively concerned in investigating his other main worry. He and Dunnet were standing outside a hotel bedroom door, with MacAlpine inserting a key in the lock. Dunnet looked around him apprehensively and said: 'I don't think the receptionist believed a word you said.'

'Who cares?' MacAlpine turned the key in the lock. 'I got Johnny's key, didn't I?'

'And if you hadn't?'

'I'd have kicked his damned door in. I've done it before, haven't I?'

The two men entered, closed and locked the door behind them. Wordlessly and methodically, they began to search Harlow's room, looking equally in the most likely as unlikely places – and in a hotel room the number of places available for concealment to even the most imaginative is very limited. Three minutes and their search was over, a search that had been as rewarding as it was deeply dismaying. The two men gazed down in a brief and almost stunned silence at the haul on

Harlow's bed – four full bottles of scotch and a fifth half full. They looked at each other and Dunnet summed up their feelings in a most succinct fashion indeed.

He said 'Jesus!'

MacAlpine nodded. Unusually for him, he seemed at a total loss for words. He didn't have to say anything for Dunnet to understand and sympathize with his feelings for the vastly unpleasant dilemma in which MacAlpine now found himself. He had committed himself to giving Harlow his last chance ever and now before him he had all the evidence he would ever require to justify Harlow's instant dismissal.

Dunnet said: 'So what do we do?'

'We take that damn poison with us, that's what we do.' MacAlpine's eyes were sick, his low voice harsh with strain.

'But he's bound to notice. And at once. From what we know of him now the first thing he'll do on return is head straight for the nearest bottle.'

'Who the hell cares what he does or notices? What can he do about it? More importantly, what can he say about it? He's not going to rush down to the desk and shout: 'I'm Johnny Harlow. Someone's just stolen five bottles of scotch from my room.' He won't be able to do or say a thing.'

'Of course he can't. But he'll still know the bottles are gone. What's he going to think about that?'

'Again, who cares what that young dipsomaniac thinks? Besides, why should it have been us.

If we had been responsible, he'd expect the heavens to fall in on him the moment he returns. But they won't. We won't say a word – yet. Could have been any thief posing as a member of the staff. Come to that, it wouldn't have been the first genuine staff member with a leaning towards petty larceny.'

'So our little bird won't sing?'

'Our little bird can't. Damn him. Damn him. Damn him.'

'Too late, my Mary,' Harlow said. 'Can't drive no more. Johnny Harlow's on the skids. Ask anyone.'

'I don't mean that and you know it. I mean your drinking.'

'Me? Drink?' Harlow's face was its usual impassive self. 'Who says that?'

'Everybody.'

'Everybody's a liar.'

As a remark, it was a guaranteed conversation-stopper. A tear fell from Mary's face on to her wrist watch but if Harlow saw it he made no comment. By and by Mary sighed and said quietly: 'I give up. I was a fool to try. Johnny, are you coming to the Mayor's reception tonight?'

'No.'

'I thought you'd like to take me. Please.'

'And make you a martyr? No.'

'Why *don't* you come? Every other race driver does.'

'I'm not every other driver. I'm Johnny Harlow. I'm a pariah, an outcast. I have a delicate and sensitive nature and I don't like it when nobody speaks to me.'

Mary put both her hands on his. 'I'll speak to you, Johnny, you know I always will.'

'I know.' Harlow spoke without either bitterness or irony. 'I cripple you for life and you'll always speak to me. Stay away from me, young Mary. I'm poison.'

'There are some poisons I could get to like very much indeed.'

Harlow squeezed her hand and rose. 'Come on. You have to get dressed for this do tonight. I'll see you back to the hotel.'

They emerged from the café, Mary using her walking stick with one hand while with the other she clung to Harlow's arm. Harlow, carrying the other stick, had slowed his normal pace to accommodate Mary's limp. As they moved slowly up the street, Rory MacAlpine emerged from the shadows of the recessed doorway opposite the café. He was shivering violently in the cold night air but seemed to be entirely unaware of this. Judging from the look of very considerable satisfaction on his face, Rory had other and more agreeable matters on his mind than the temperature. He crossed the street, followed Harlow and Mary at a discreet distance until he came to the first road junction. He turned right into this and began to run.

By the time he had arrived back at the hotel, he was no longer shivering but sweating profusely for he had not stopped running all the way. He slowed down to cross the lobby and mount the stairs, went to his room, washed, combed his hair, straightened his tie, spent a few moments in front of his mirror practising his sad but dutiful expression until he thought he had it about right, then walked across towards his father's room. He knocked, received some sort of mumbled reply and went inside.

James MacAlpine's suite was, by any odds, the most comfortable in the hotel. As a millionaire, MacAlpine could afford to indulge himself: as both a man and a millionaire he saw no reason why he shouldn't. But MacAlpine wasn't indulging in any indulgence at that moment, nor, as he sat far back in an over-stuffed armchair did he appear to be savouring any of the creature comforts surrounding him. He appeared, instead, to be sunk in some deep and private gloom from which he roused himself enough to look up almost apathetically as his son closed the door behind him.

'Well, my boy, what is it? Couldn't it wait until the morning?'

'No, Dad, it couldn't.'

'Out with it, then. You can see I'm busy.'

'Yes, Dad, I know.' Rory's sad but dutiful expression remained in position. 'But there's something I felt I had to tell you.' He hesitated as if embarrassed at what he was about to say. 'It's about Johnny Harlow, Dad.'

'Anything you have to say about Harlow will be treated with the greatest reserve.' Despite the words, a degree of interest had crept into MacAlpine's thinning features. 'We all know what you think of Harlow.'

'Yes, Dad. I thought of that before I came to see you.' Rory hesitated again. 'You know this thing about Johnny Harlow, Dad? The stories people are telling about his drinking too much.'

'Well?' MacAlpine's tone was wholly non-committal. It was with some difficulty that Rory managed to keep his pious expression from slipping: this was going to be much more difficult than he expected.

'It's true. The drinking, I mean. I saw him in a pub tonight.'

'Thank you, Rory, you may go.' He paused. 'Were you in that pub too?'

'Me? Come on, Dad. I was outside. I could see in, though.'

'Spying, lad?'

'I was passing by.' A curt but injured tone.

MacAlpine waved a hand in dismissal. Rory turned to go, then turned again to face his father.

'Maybe I don't like Johnny Harlow. But I do like Mary. I like her more than any person in the world.' MacAlpine nodded, he knew this to be true. 'I don't ever want to see her hurt. That's why I came to see you. She was in that pub with Harlow.'

'What!' MacAlpine's face had darkened in immediate anger.

'Cut my throat and hope I die.'

'You are sure?'

'I *am* sure, Dad. Of course I'm sure. Nothing wrong with my eyes.'

'I'm sure there's not.' MacAlpine said mechanically. A little, but not much, of the anger had left his eyes. 'It's just that I don't want to accept it. Mind you, I don't like spying.'

'This wasn't spying, Dad.' Rory's indignation could be of a particularly nauseating righteousness at times. 'This was detective work. When the good name of the Coronado team is at stake – '

MacAlpine lifted his hand to stop the spate of words and sighed heavily.

'All right, all right, you virtuous little monster. Tell Mary I want her. Now. But don't tell her why.'

Five minutes later Rory had been replaced by a Mary who looked simultaneously apprehensive and defiant. She said: 'Who told you this?'

'Never mind who told me. Is it true or not?'

'I'm twenty-two, Daddy.' She was very quiet. 'I don't have to answer you. I can look after myself.'

'Can you? Can you? If I were to throw you off the Coronado team? You've no money and you won't have till I'm dead. You've got no place to go. You've no mother now, at least no mother you can reach. You've no qualifications for anything. Who's going to employ a cripple without qualifications?'

'I would like to hear you say those horrible things to me in front of Johnny Harlow.'

'Surprisingly, perhaps, I won't react to that one. I was just as independent at your age, more so, I guess, and taking a poor view of parental authority.' He paused, then went on curiously: 'You in love with this fellow?'

'He's not a fellow. He's Johnny Harlow.' MacAlpine raised an eyebrow at the intensity in her voice. 'As for your question, am I never to be allowed any areas of privacy in my life?'

'All right, all right.' MacAlpine sighed. 'A deal. If you answer my questions then I'll tell you why I'm asking them. OK?'

She nodded.

'Fine. True or false?'

'If your spies are certain of their facts, Daddy, then why bother asking me?'

'Mind your tongue.' The reference to spies had touched MacAlpine to the raw.

'Apologize for saying "mind your tongue" to me.'

'Jesus!' MacAlpine looked at his daughter in an astonishment that was compounded half of irritation, half of admiration. 'You must be my daughter. I apologize. Did he drink?'

'Yes.'

'What?'

'I don't know. Something clear. He said it was tonic and water.'

'And that's the kind of liar you keep company with. Tonic and bloody water! Stay away from him, Mary. If you don't, it's back home to Marseille for you.'

'Why, Daddy? Why? Why? Why?'

'Because God knows I've got enough trouble of my own without having my only daughter tying herself up to an alcoholic with the skids under him.'

'Johnny! Alcoholic! Look, Daddy, I know he drinks a little – '

MacAlpine silenced her by the gesture of picking up the phone.

'MacAlpine here. Will you ask Mr Dunnet to come to see me? Yes. Now.' He replaced the phone. 'I said I'd tell you why I was asking those questions. I didn't want to. But I'm going to have to.'

Dunnet entered and closed the door behind him. He had about him the look of a man who was not looking forward too keenly to the next few minutes. After asking Dunnet to sit down he said: 'Tell her, Alexis, would you, please?'

Dunnet looked even more acutely unhappy. 'Must I, James?'

'I'm afraid so. She'd never believe me if I told her what we found in Johnny's room.'

Mary looked at each in turn, sheer incredulity in her face. 'She said: 'You were searching Johnny's room.'

Dunnet took a deep breath. 'With good reason, Mary, and thank God we did. I can still hardly believe it myself. We found five bottles of scotch hidden in his room. One of them was half empty.'

Mary looked at them, stricken. Clearly, she believed them all too well. When MacAlpine spoke, it was very gently.

'I *am* sorry. We all know how fond you are of him. We took the bottles away, incidentally.'

'You took the bottles away.' Her voice was slow and dull and uncomprehending. 'But he'll know. He'll report the theft. There'll be police. There'll be fingerprints – your fingerprints. Then – '

MacAlpine said: 'Can you imagine Johnny Harlow ever admitting to anyone in the world that he'd five bottles of scotch in his room? Run along, girl, and get dressed. We've got to leave for this bloody reception in twenty minutes – without, it seems, your precious Johnny.'

She remained seated, her face quite without expression, her unblinking eyes irremovably fixed on MacAlpine's. After a few moments his expression softened and he smiled. He said: 'I'm sorry. That was quite uncalled for.'

Dunnet held the door while she hobbled from the room. Both men watched her go with pity in their eyes.

CHAPTER FIVE

To the Grand Prix racing fraternity of the world, as to seasoned travellers everywhere, a hotel is a hotel is a hotel, a place to sleep, a place to eat, a stopover to the next faceless anonymity. The newly-built Villa-Hotel Cessni on the outskirts of Monza, however, could fairly claim to be an exception to the truism. Superbly designed, superbly built and superbly landscaped, its huge airy rooms with their immaculately designed furniture, their luxurious bathrooms, splendidly sweeping balconies, sumptuous food and warmth of service, here one would have thought was the caravanserai nonpareil for the better-heeled millionaire.

And so it would be, one day, but not yet. The Villa-Hotel Cessni had as yet to establish its clientele, its image, its reputation and, hopefully and eventually, its traditions and for the achievement of those infinitely desirable ends, the fair uses of publicity, for luxury hotels as for hotdog stands, could be very sweet indeed. No sport on earth has a more international following and it was with this in mind that the management had deemed it prudent to invite the major Grand Prix teams to accommodate themselves in this palace, for a ludicrously low nominal fee, for the duration of the Italian Grand Prix. Few teams had failed to accept the invitation and fewer still cared to exercise their minds with the philosophical and psychological motivations of the management: all they knew and cared about was that the Hotel-Villa Cessni was infinitely more luxurious and fractionally cheaper than the several Austrian hotels they had so gratefully abandoned only twelve days ago. Next year, it seemed likely, they wouldn't even be allowed to sleep stacked six-deep in the basement: but that was next year.

That Friday evening late in August was warm but by no means warm enough to justify air-conditioning. Nevertheless, the air-conditioning in the lobby of the Hotel-Villa Cessni was operating at the top of its bent making the temperature in that luxuriously appointed haven from the lower classes almost uncomfortably cool. Common sense said that this interior climatic condition was wholly unnecessary: the prestige of an up and coming status symbol said that it was wholly necessary. The management was concerned with prestige to the point of obsession: the air-conditioning remained on. The Cessni was going to be the place to go when the sun rode high.

MacAlpine and Dunnet, sitting side by side but almost concealed from each other's sight by virtue of the imposing construction of the vast velvet-lined arm-chairs in which they reclined rather than sat, had more important things on their minds than a few degrees of temperature hither and yonder. They spoke but seldom and then with a marked lack of animation: they gave the air of those who had precious little to get animated about. Dunnet stirred.

'Our wandering boy is late on the road tonight.'

'He has an excuse,' MacAlpine said. 'At least, I hope to hell he has. One thing, he was always a conscientious workman. He wanted a few more extra laps to adjust the suspension and gear ratios of this new car of his.'

Dunnet was gloomy. 'It wouldn't have been possible, I suppose, to give it to Tracchia instead?'

'Quite impossible, Alexis, and you know it. The mighty law of protocol. Johnny's not only Coronado's number one, he's still the world's. Our dear sponsors, without which we couldn't very well operate – I could, but I'll be damned if I'll lay out a fortune like that – are highly sensitive people. Sensitive to public opinion, that is. The only reason they paint the names of their damned products on the outside of our cars is that the public will go out and buy those same damned products. They're not benefactors of racing except purely incidentally: they are simply advertisers. An advertiser wants to reach the biggest market. Ninety-nine point repeater nine per cent of that market lies outside the racing world and it doesn't matter a damn if they know nothing about what goes on inside the racing world. It's what they believe that matters. And they believe that Harlow still stands alone. So, Harlow gets the best and newest car. If he doesn't, the public lose their faith in Harlow, in Coronado and in the advertisers, and not necessarily in that order.'

'Ah, well. The days of miracles may not yet lie behind us. After all, he hasn't been observed or known to take a drink in the past twelve days. Maybe he's going to surprise us all. And there's only two days to go to the Italian Grand Prix.'

'So why did he have those two bottles of scotch which you removed from his room only an hour ago?'

'I could say he was trying to test his moral fibre but I don't think you would believe it.'

'Would you?'

'Frankly, James, no.' Dunnet relapsed into another period of gloom from which he emerged to say: 'Any word from your agents in the south, James?'

'Nothing. I'm afraid, Alexis, I've just about given up hope. Fourteen weeks now since Marie disappeared. It's too long, it's just too long. Had there been an accident, I would have heard. Had there been foul play, then I'm sure I would have heard. Had it been kidnap and ransom – well, that's ridiculous, of course I would have heard. She's just vanished. Accident, boating – I don't know.'

'And we've talked so often about amnesia.'

'And I've told you so often, without immodesty, that no one as well known as Marie MacAlpine, no matter what her mental trouble, could go missing so long without being picked up.'

'I know. Mary's taking that pretty badly now, isn't she?'

'Especially in the past twelve days. Harlow. Alexis, we broke her heart – sorry, that's quite unfair – *I* broke her heart in Austria. If I'd known how far she was gone – ah, but I'd no option.'

'Taking her to the reception tonight?'

'Yes. I insisted. To take her out of herself, that's what I tell *my*self – or is it just to ease my conscience? Again, I don't know. Maybe I'm making another mistake.'

'It seems to me that that young fellow Harlow has a great deal to answer for. And this is his last chance, James? Any more crazy driving, any more fiascos, any more drinking – then it's the chopper? That's it?'

'That's entirely it.' MacAlpine nodded in the direction of the revolving entrance doors. 'Think we should tell him now?'

Dunnet looked in the direction indicated. Harlow was walking across the Carrara-marbled flags. He was still clad in his customarily immaculate white racing overalls. A young and rather beautiful young girl at the desk smiled at him as he passed by. Harlow flicked her an expressionless glance and the smile froze. He continued on his way across the vast lobby and such is the respect that men accord the gods when they walk the earth that a hundred conversations died as he passed by. Harlow seemed unaware of the presence of any of them, for he looked neither to left nor to right, but it was a safe assumption that those remarkable eyes missed nothing, an assumption borne out by the fact that, apparently without noticing them, he veered direction towards where MacAlpine and Dunnet sat. MacAlpine said: 'No scotch or menthol, that's for sure. Otherwise, he'd avoid me like the plague.'

Harlow stood before them. He said, without any inflection of irony or sarcasm: 'Enjoying the quiet evenfall, gentlemen?'

MacAlpine answered. 'You could say that. We might enjoy it even more if you could tell us how the new Coronado is coming along.'

'Shaping up. Jacobson – for once – agrees with me that a slight alteration in the ratios and the rear suspension is all that's necessary. It'll be all right for Sunday.'

'No complaints, then?'

'No. It's a fine car. Best Coronado yet. And fast'

'How fast?'

'I haven't found out yet. But we equalled the lap record the last two times out.'

'Well, well.' MacAlpine looked at his watch. 'Better hurry. We have to leave for the reception in half an hour.'

'I'm tired. I'm going to have a shower, two hours' sleep, then some dinner. I've come here for the Grand Prix, not for mingling with high society.'

'You definitely refuse to come?'

'I refused to come last time out too. Setting a precedent, if you like.'

'It's obligatory, you know.'

'In my vocabulary, obligation and compulsion are not the same things.'

'There are three or four very important people present tonight especially just to see you.'

'I know.'

MacAlpine paused before speaking. 'How do you know. Only Alexis and I know.'

'Mary told me.' Harlow turned and walked away.

'Well.' Dunnet pressed his lips tightly together. 'The arrogant young bastard. Walking in here to tell us he's just equalled the lap record without even trying. Thing is, I believe him. That's why he stopped by, isn't it?'

'To tell me that he's still the best in the business? Partly. Also to tell me to stuff my bloody reception. Also to tell me that he'll speak to Mary whether I like it or not. And the final twist, to let me know that Mary has no secrets from him. Where's that damned daughter of mine?'

'This should be interesting to see.'

'What should be?'

'To see if you can break a heart twice.'

MacAlpine sighed and slumped even farther back in his arm-chair. 'I suppose you're right, Alexis, I suppose you're right. Mind you, I'd still like to knock their two damned young heads together.'

Harlow, clad in a white bath-robe and obviously recently showered, emerged from the bathroom and opened up his wardrobe. He brought out a fresh suit then reached up to a shelf above it. Clearly, he didn't find what he expected to and his eyebrows lifted. He looked in a cupboard with similarly negative results. He stood in the middle of the room, pondering, then smiled widely.

He said softly: 'Well, well, well. Here we go again. Clever devils.'

From the still-smiling expression on his face, it was clear that Harlow didn't believe his own words. He lifted the mattress, reached under, removed a flat half-bottle of scotch, examined and replaced it. From there he went into the bathroom, removed the cistern lid, lifted out a bottle of Glenfiddich malt, checked the level – it was about three-parts full, replaced it in a certain position and then put the cistern lid back in place. This he left slightly askew. He returned to his bedroom, put on a light grey suit and was just adjusting his tie when he heard the sound of a heavy engine below. He switched out the light, pulled back the curtains, opened his window and peered out cautiously.

A large coach was drawn up outside the hotel entrance and the various drivers, managers, senior mechanics and journalists who were headed for the official reception were filing aboard. Harlow checked to see that all those whose absence that evening he considered highly desirable were among those present, and they were – Dunnet, Tracchia, Neubauer, Jacobson and MacAlpine, the last with a very pale and downcast Mary clinging to his arm. The door closed and the bus moved off into the night.

Five minutes later, Harlow sauntered up to the reception desk. Behind it was the very pretty young girl he'd ignored on the way in. He smiled widely at her – his colleagues wouldn't have believed it – and she, recovering quickly from the shock of seeing the other side of Harlow's nature, smiled in return, almost blushing in embarrassed pleasure. For those outside immediate racing circles, Harlow was still the world's number one.

Harlow said: 'Good evening.'

'Good evening, Mr Harlow, sir.' The smile faded. 'I'm afraid you've just missed your bus.'

'I have my own private transport.'

The smile came back on again. 'Of course, Mr Harlow. How silly of me. Your red Ferrari. Is there something – '

'Yes, please. I have four names here – MacAlpine, Neubauer, Tracchia and Jacobson. I wonder if you could give me their room numbers?'

'Certainly, Mr Harlow. But I'm afraid those gentlemen have all just left.'

'I know. I *waited* until they had left.'

'I don't understand, sir.'

'I just want to slip something under their doors. An old pre-race custom.'

'You race drivers and your practical jokes.' She'd almost certainly never seen a race driver until that evening but that didn't prevent her from giving him a look of roguish understanding. 'The numbers you want are 202, 208, 204 and 206.'

'That's in the order of the names I gave you?'

'Yes, sir.'

'Thank you.' Harlow touched a finger to his lips. 'Now, not a word.'

'Of *course* not, Mr Harlow.' She smiled conspiratorially at him as he turned away. Harlow had a sufficiently realistic assessment of his own fame to appreciate that she would talk for months about this brief encounter: just as long as she didn't talk until that weekend was over.

He returned to his own room, took a movie camera from a suitcase, unscrewed its back, carefully scratching the dull metallic black as he did so, removed the plate and pulled out a small miniaturized camera not much larger than a packet of cigarettes. He pocketed this, rescrewed in place the back plate of the movie camera, replaced it in his suitcase and looked thoughtfully at the small canvas bag of tools that lay there. Tonight, he would not require those: where he was going he knew where to find all the tools and flash-lights he wanted. He took the bag with him and left the room.

He moved along the corridor to room 202 – MacAlpine's room. Unlike MacAlpine, Harlow did not have to resort to devious means to obtain hotel room keys – he had some excellent sets of keys himself. He selected one of these and with the fourth key the door opened. He entered and locked the door behind him.

Having disposed of the canvas bag in the highest and virtually unreachable shelf in a wall wardrobe, Harlow proceeded to search the room thoroughly. Nothing escaped his scrutiny – MacAlpine's clothing, wardrobes, cupboards, suitcases. Finally he came across a locked suitcase, so small as to be almost a brief-case, fastened with locks that were very strong and peculiar indeed. But Harlow also had a set of very small and peculiar keys. Opening the small suitcase presented no difficulty whatsoever.

The interior held a kind of small travelling office, containing as it did a mass of papers, including invoices, receipts, cheque-books and contracts: the owner of the Coronado team obviously served as his own accountant. Harlow ignored everything except an elastic-bound bunch of expired cheque-books. He flipped through those quickly then stopped and stared at the front few pages of one of the cheque-books where all the payments were recorded together. He examined all four recording pages closely, shook his head in evident disbelief, pursed his lips in a soundless whistle, brought out his miniature camera and took eight pictures, two of each page. This done, he returned everything as he had found it and left.

The corridor was deserted. Harlow moved down to 204 – Tracchia's room – and used the same key to enter as he had on MacAlpine's door: hotel room keys have only marginal differences as they have to accommodate a master key: what Harlow had was, in fact, a master key.

As Tracchia had considerably fewer possessions than MacAlpine, the search was correspondingly easier. Again Harlow encountered another, but smaller, brief-case, the opening of which again provided him with the minimum of difficulty. There were but few papers inside and Harlow found little of interest among them except a thin book, bound in black and red, of what appeared to be a list of extremely cryptic addresses. Each address, if address it were, was headed by a single letter, followed by two or three wholly indecipherable lines of letters. It could have meant something: it could have meant nothing. Harlow hesitated, obviously in a state of indecision, shrugged, brought out his camera and photographed the pages. He left

Tracchia.'s room in as immaculate a condition as he had left MacAlpine's.

Two minutes later in 208, Harlow, sitting on Neubauer's bed with a brief-case on his lap, was no longer hesitating. The miniature camera clicked busily away: the thin black and red note-book he held in his hand was identical to the one he had found in Tracchia's possession.

From there, Harlow moved on to the last of his four objectives – Jacobson's room. Jacobson, it appeared, was either less discreet or less sophisticated than either Tracchia or Neubauer. He had two bank-books and when Harlow opened them he sat quite still. Jacobson's income, it appeared from them, amounted to at least twenty times as much as he could reasonably expect to earn as a chief mechanic. Inside one of the books was a list of addresses, in plain English, scattered all over Europe. All those details Harlow faithfully recorded on his little camera. He replaced the papers in the case and the case in its original position and was on the point of leaving when he heard footsteps in the corridor. He stood, irresolute, until the footsteps came to a halt outside his door. He pulled a handkerchief from his pocket and was about to use it as a mask when a key turned in the lock. Harlow had time only to move swiftly and silently into a wardrobe,pulling the door quietly to behind him, when the corridor door opened and someone entered the room.

From where Harlow was, all was total darkness. He could hear someone moving around the room but had no idea from the sound as to what the source of the activity might be: for all he could tell someone might have been engaged in exactly the same pursuit as he himself had been a minute ago. Working purely by feel, he folded his handkerchief cornerwise, adjusted the straight edge to a point just below his eyes and knotted the handkerchief behind the back of his head.

The wardrobe door opened and Harlow was confronted with the spectacle of a portly, middle-aged chambermaid carrying a bolster in her hands – she'd obviously just been changing it for the nighttime pillows. She, in turn, was confronted with the shadowy menacing figure of a man in a white mask. The chambermaid's eyes turned up in her head. Soundlessly, without even as much as a sigh, she swayed and crumpled slowly towards the floor. Harlow stepped out, caught her before she hit the marble tiles and lowered her gently, using the bolster as a pillow. He moved quickly towards the opened corridor door, closed it, removed his handkerchief and proceeded to wipe all the surfaces he had touched, including the top and handle of the brief-case. Finally, he took the telephone off the hook and left it lying on the table. He left, pulling the door to behind him but not quite closing it.

He passed swiftly along the corridor, descended the stairs at a leisurely pace, went to the bar and ordered himself a drink. The barman looked at him in what came to being open astonishment.

'You said what, sir?'

'Double gin and tonic is what I said.'

'Yes, Mr Harlow. Very good, Mr Harlow.'

As impassively as he could, the barman prepared the drink which Harlow took to a wall seat situated between two potted plants. He looked across the lobby with interest. There were some signs of unusual activity at the telephone switchboard, where the girl operator was showing increasing signs of irritation. A light on her board kept flashing on and off but she was obviously having no success in contacting the room number in question. Finally, clearly exasperated, she beckoned a page boy and said something in a low voice. The page boy nodded and crossed the lobby at the properly sedate pace in keeping with the advertised ambience of the Hotel-Villa Cessni.

When he returned, it was at anything but a sedate pace. He ran across the lobby and whispered something urgently to the operator. She left her seat and only seconds later no less a personage than the manager himself appeared and hurried across the lobby. Harlow waited patiently, pretending to sip his drink from time to time. He knew that most people in the lobby were covertly studying him but was unconcerned. From where they sat he was drinking a harmless lemonade or tonic water. The barman, of course, knew better and it was as certain as that night's sundown that one of the first things that MacAlpine would do on his return would be to ask for Johnny Harlow's drink bill, on the convincing enough pretext that it was inconceivable for the champion to put his hand in his pocket for anything.

The manager reappeared, moving with most unmanagerial haste, in a sort of disciplined trot, reached the desk and busied himself with the telephone. The entire lobby was now agog with interest and expectation. Their undivided attention had now been transferred from Harlow to the front desk and Harlow took advantage of this to tip the contents of his glass into a potted plant. He rose and sauntered across the lobby as if heading for the front revolving doors. His route brought him past the side of the manager. Harlow broke step.

He said sympathetically: 'Trouble?'

'Grave trouble, Mr Harlow. Very grave.' The manager had the phone to his ear, obviously waiting for a call to come through, but it was still apparent that he was flattered that Johnny Harlow should take time off to speak to him. 'Burglars! Assassins! One of our chambermaids has been most brutally and savagely assaulted.'

'Good God! Where?'

'Mr Jacobson's room.'

'Jacobson's – but he's only our chief mechanic. He's got nothing worth stealing.'

'Ah! Like enough, Mr Harlow. But the burglar wasn't to know that, was he?'

Harlow said anxiously: 'I hope she was able to identify her attacker.'

'Impossible. All she remembers is a masked giant jumping out of a wardrobe and attacking her. He was carrying a club, she said.' He put his hand over the mouthpiece. 'Excuse me. The police.'

Harlow turned, exhaled a long slow sigh of relief, walked away, passed out through the revolving doors, turned right and then right again, re-entered the hotel through one of the side doors and made his way unobserved back up to his own room. Here he withdrew the sealed film cassette from his miniature camera, replaced it with a fresh one – or one that appeared to be fresh – unscrewed the back of his cine-camera, inserted the miniature and screwed home the back plate of the cine-camera. For good measure, he added a few more scratches to the dulled black metal finish. The original cassette he put in an envelope, wrote on it his name and room number, took it down to the desk, where the more immediate signs of panic appeared to be over, asked that it be put in the safe and returned to his room.

An hour later, Harlow, his more conventional wear now replaced by a navy roll-neck pullover and leather jacket, sat waiting patiently on the edge of his bed. For the second time that night, he heard the sound of a heavy diesel motor outside, for the second time that night he switched off the light, pulled the curtains, opened the window and looked out. The reception party bus had returned. He pulled the curtains to again, switched on the light, removed the flat bottle of scotch from under the mattress, rinsed his mouth with some of it and left.

He was descending the foot of the stairs as the reception party entered the lobby. Mary, reduced to only one stick now, was on her father's arm but when MacAlpine saw Harlow he handed her to Dunnet. Mary looked at Harlow quietly and steadily but her face didn't say anything.

Harlow made to brush by but MacAlpine barred his way.

MacAlpine said: 'The mayor was very vexed and displeased by your absence.'

Harlow seemed totally unconcerned by the mayor's reactions. He said: 'I'll bet he was the only one.'

'You remember you have some practice laps first thing in the morning?'

'I'm the person who has to do them. Is it likely that I would forget?'

Harlow made to move by MacAlpine but the latter blocked his way again.

MacAlpine said: 'Where are you going?'

'Out.'

'I forbid you – '

'You'll forbid me nothing that isn't in my contract.'

Harlow left. Dunnet looked at MacAlpine and sniffed.

'Air *is* a bit thick, isn't it?'

'We missed something,' MacAlpine said. 'We'd better go and see what it was we missed.'

Mary looked at them in turn.

'So you've already searched his room when he was out on the track. And now that his back is turned again you're going to search it again. Despicable. Utterly despicable. You're nothing better than a couple of – a couple of sneak-thieves.' She pulled her arm away from Dunnet. 'Leave me alone. I can find my own room.'

Both men watched her limp across the foyer. Dunnet said complainingly: 'Considering the issues involved, life or death issues, if you like, I do consider that a rather unreasonable attitude.'

'So is love,' MacAlpine sighed. 'So is love.'

Harlow, descending the hotel steps, brushed by Neubauer and Tracchia. Not only did he not speak to them, for they still remained on courtesy terms, he didn't even appear to see them. Both men turned and looked after Harlow. He was walking with that over-erect, over-stiff posture of the slightly inebriated who are making too good a job of trying to pretend that all is well. Even as they watched, Harlow made one barely perceptible and clearly unpremeditated stagger to one side, but quickly recovered and was back on an over-straight course again. Neubauer and Tracchia exchanged glances, nodded to each other briefly, just once. Neubauer went into the hotel while Tracchia moved off after Harlow.

The earlier warm night air had suddenly begun to chill, the coolness being accompanied by a slight drizzle. This was to Tracchia's advantage. City-dwellers are notoriously averse to anything more than a slight humidity in the atmosphere, and although the Hotel-Villa Cessni was situated in what was really nothing more than a small village, the same urban principle applied: with the first signs of rain the streets began to clear rapidly: the danger of losing Harlow among crowds of people decreased almost to nothingness. The rain increased steadily until finally Tracchia was following Harlow through almost deserted streets. This, of course, increased the chances of detection should Harlow choose to cast a backward glance but it became quickly evident that Harlow had no intention of casting any backward glances: he had about him the fixed and determined air of a man who was heading for a certain objective and backward glances were no part of his forward-looking plans. Tracchia, sensing this, began to move up closer until he was no more than ten yards behind Harlow.

Harlow's behaviour was becoming steadily more erratic. He had lost his ability to pursue a straight line and was beginning to weave noticeably. On one occasion he staggered in against a recessed doorway shop window and Tracchia caught a glimpse of Harlow's reflected face, head shaking and eyes apparently closed. But he pushed himself off and went resolutely if unsteadily on his way.

Tracchia closed up even more, his face registering an expression of mingled amusement, contempt and disgust. The expression deepened as Harlow, his condition still deteriorating, lurched round a street corner to his left.

Temporarily out of Tracchia's line of vision, Harlow, all signs of insobriety vanished, moved rapidly into the first darkened doorway round the corner. From a back pocket he withdrew an article not normally carried by racing drivers – a woven leather black-jack with a wrist thong. Harlow slipped the thong over his hand and waited.

He had little enough time to wait. As Tracchia rounded the corner the contempt on his face gave way to consternation when he saw that the ill-lit street ahead was empty. Anxiously, he increased his pace and within half a dozen paces was passing by the shadowed and recessed doorway where Harlow waited.

A Grand Prix driver needs timing, accuracy and eyesight. All of those Harlow had in superabundance. Also he was extremely fit. Tracchia lost consciousness instantly. Without as much as a glance at it, Harlow stepped over the prostrate body and strode briskly on his way. Only, it wasn't the way he had been going. He retraced his tracks for about a quarter of a mile, turned left and almost at once found himself in the transporter parking lot. It seemed extremely unlikely that Tracchia, when he came to, would have even the slightest idea as to where Harlow had been headed.

Harlow made directly for the nearest transporter. Even through the rain and near darkness the name, in two feet high golden letters, was easily distinguishable: CORONADO. He unlocked the door, passed inside and switched on the lights and very powerful lights they were too, as they had to be for mechanics working on such delicate engineering. Here there was no need for glowing red lights, stealth and secrecy: there was no one who was going to question Johnny Harlow's right to be inside his own transporter. Nevertheless, he took the precaution of locking the door from the inside and leaving the key half-turned in the lock so that it couldn't be opened from the outside. Then he used ply to mask the windows so that he couldn't be seen from outside: only then did he make for the tool-rack on the side and select the implements he wanted.

MacAlpine and Dunnet, not for the first time, were illegally in Harlow's room and not feeling too happy about it: not about the illegality but what they had found there. More precisely, they were in Harlow's bathroom. Dunnet had the cistern cover in his hand while MacAlpine held up a dripping bottle of malt whisky. Both men regarded each other, at a momentary loss for words, then Dunnet said: 'Resourceful lad is our Johnny. He's probably got a crate hidden under the driving seat of his Coronado. But I think you'd better leave that bottle where you found it.'

'Why ever should I? What's the point in that?'

'That way we *may* know his daily consumption. If he can't get it from that bottle he'll sure as hell get it elsewhere – you know his uncanny way of vanishing in that red Ferrari of his. And then we'll never know how much he drinks.'

'I suppose so, I suppose so.' He looked at the bottle and there was pain in his eyes. 'The most gifted driver of our time, perhaps the most gifted driver of all time, and now it's come to this. Why do the gods strike a man like Johnny Harlow down, Alexis? Because he's beginning to walk too close to them.'

'Put the bottle back, James.'

Only two doors away was another pair of unhappy men, one of them markedly so. Tracchia, from the incessant way in which he massaged the back of his neck, appeared to be in very considerable pain. Neubauer watched him with a mixture of sympathy and anger.

Neubauer said: 'Sure it was that bastard Harlow?'

'I'm sure. I've still got my wallet.'

'That was careless of him. I think I'll lose my room key and borrow the master.'

Tracchia momentarily ceased to massage his aching neck. 'What the hell for?'

'You'll see. Stay here.'

Neubauer returned within two minutes, a key ring whirling round his finger. He said: 'I'm taking the blonde at reception out on Sunday night. I think I'll ask for the keys of the safe next time.'

Tracchia said in agonized patience: 'Willi, there is a time and a place for comedy.'

'Sorry.' He opened the door and they passed out into the corridor. It was deserted. Less than ten seconds later they were both inside Harlow's room, the door locked behind them.

Tracchia said: 'What happens if Harlow comes along?'

'Who would you rather be? Harlow or us?'

They had spent no more than a minute in searching when Neubauer suddenly said: 'You were quite right, Nikki. Our dear friend Johnny *is* just that little bit careless.'

He showed Tracchia the cine-camera with the crisscross of scratches round each of the four screws securing the plate at the back, produced a pocket-knife, selected a small screw-driver, removed the plate and extracted the micro camera. Neubauer then extracted the cassette from the micro camera and examined it thoughtfully. He said: 'We take this?'

Tracchia shook his head and instantly screwed up his face in the agony caused by the thoughtless movement. When he had recovered, he said: 'No. He would have known we were here.'

Neubauer said: 'So there's only one thing for it then?'

Tracchia nodded and again winced in pain. Neubauer lifted off the cover of the cassette, unreeled the film and passed it under a strong desk lamp, then, not without some difficulty, rewound the film, replaced the cover, put the cassette back in the micro camera and the micro camera in the cine.

Tracchia said: 'This proves nothing. We contact Marseilles?'

Neubauer nodded. Both men left the room.

Harlow had a Coronado pushed back by about a foot. He peered at the section of floor-board revealed, reached for a powerful torch, knelt and examined the floor intently. One of the longitudinal planks appeared to have two transverse lines on it, about fifteen inches apart. Harlow used an oily cloth to rub the front line, whereupon it became evident that the front line was no line at all but a very fine sharp cut. The revealed heads of the two holding nails were bright and clear of any marks. Harlow brought a chisel to bear and the front of the inlet wooden section lifted with surprising ease. He reached down an arm to explore the depth and length of the space beneath. A fractional lifting of the eyebrows expressed some degree of surprise, almost certainly as to the unseen extent of area available. Harlow brought out his arm and touched fingertips to mouth and nose: there was no perceptible change in his expression. He replaced the board section and gently tapped it into place, using the butt of a chisel on the gleaming nail-heads. With a suitably oiled and dirty cloth he smeared the cuts and nails.

Forty-five minutes had elapsed between the time of Harlow's departure from the Villa-Hotel Cessni and his return there. The vast foyer looked semi-deserted but there must, in fact, have been over a hundred people there, many of them from the official reception party, all of them, probably, waiting to go in for late dinner. The first two people Harlow saw were MacAlpine and Dunnet, sitting alone at a small table with short drinks. Two tables away Mary sat by herself, a soft drink and a magazine in front of her. She didn't give the impression of reading and there was a certain stiff aloofness in her bearing. Harlow wondered towards whom the hostility was directed. Towards himself, likely enough, but on the other hand there had grown up an increasing estrangement between Mary on the one hand and MacAlpine on the other. Of Rory there was no sign. Probably out spying somewhere, Harlow thought.

The three of them caught sight of Harlow at almost the same instant as he saw them. MacAlpine immediately rose to his feet.

'I'd be grateful, Alexis, if you could take Mary in to dinner. I'm going into the dining-room. I'm afraid if I were to stay – '

'It's all right, James. I understand.'

Harlow watched the calculated snub of the departing back without expression, an absence of outward feeling that quickly changed to a certain apprehension as he saw Mary bearing down on him. No question now as to whom the unspoken hostility had been directed. She gave the very distinct impression of having been waiting for him. That bewitching smile that had made her the sweetheart of the race-tracks was, Harlow observed, in marked abeyance. He braced himself for what he knew was going to be a low but correspondingly fierce voice.

'Must you let *everybody* see you like this? And in a *place* like this.' Harlow frowned in puzzlement. 'You've been at it again.'

He said: 'That's right. Go ahead. Wound an innocent man's feelings. You have my worded bond – I mean my bonded word – '

'It's disgusting! Sober men don't fall flat on their faces in the street. Look at the state of your clothes, your filthy hands. Go on ! Just *look* at yourself.'

Harlow looked at himself.

'Oh! Aha! Well, sweet dreams, sweet Mary.'

He turned towards the stairs, took five steps and halted abruptly when confronted by Dunnet. For a moment the two men looked at each other, faces immobile, then there was an almost imperceptible lift of Dunnet's eyebrow. When Harlow spoke, his voice was very quiet.

He said: 'We go now.'

'The Coronado?'

'Yes.'

'We go now.'

CHAPTER SIX

Harlow drained his coffee – it was by now his invariable custom to breakfast alone in his bedroom – and crossed to the window. The famed Italian September sun was nowhere to be seen that morning. The overcast was very heavy, but the ground was dry and the visibility excellent, a combination making for ideal race-track conditions. He went into the bathroom, opened the window to its fullest extent, removed the cistern cover, took out the scotch, turned on the hot water tap and systematically poured half the contents of the bottle into the basin. He returned the bottle to its hiding-place, sprayed the room very heavily with an airfresh aerosol and left.

He drove alone to the race-track – the passenger seat in his red Ferrari was rarely occupied now – to find Jacobson, his two mechanics and Dunnet already there. He greeted them briefly and in very short order, overalled and helmeted, was sitting in the cockpit of his new Coronado. Jacobson favoured him with his usual grimly despondent look.

He said: 'I hope you can give us good practice lap-time today, Johnny.'

Harlow said mildly: 'I thought I didn't do too badly yesterday. However, one can but try.' With his finger on the starter button he glanced at Dunnet. 'And where is our worthy employer today? Never known him to miss a practice lap before.'

'In the hotel. He has things to attend to.'

MacAlpine did, indeed, have things to attend to. What he was attending to at that moment had by this time become almost a routine chore – investigating the current level of Harlow's alcohol supply. As soon as he entered Harlow's bathroom he realized that checking the level of scotch in the bottle in the cistern was going to be a mere formality: the wide open window and the air heavy with the scent of the aerosol spray made further investigation almost superfluous. However, investigate he did: even though he had been almost certain what to expect, his face still darkened with anger as he held the half empty bottle up for inspection. He replaced the bottle, left Harlow's room almost at a run, actually ran across the hotel foyer, climbed into his Aston and drove off in a fashion that might well have left the astonished onlookers with the impression that he had mistaken the forecourt of the Villa-Hotel Cessni for the Monza circuit.

MacAlpine was still running when he arrived at the Coronado pits: there he encountered Dunnet who was just leaving them. MacAlpine was panting heavily. He said: 'Where's that young bastard Harlow?'

Dunnet did not reply at once. He seemed more concerned with shaking his head slowly from side to side.

'God's sake, man, where's that drunken layabout?' MacAlpine's voice was almost a shout. 'He mustn't be allowed anywhere near that damned track.'

'There's a lot of other drivers in Monza who would agree with you.'

'What's that meant to mean?'

'It means that that drunken layabout has just broken the lap record by two point one seconds.' Dunnet continued to shake his head in continued disbelief. 'Bloody well incredible.'

'Two point one! Two point one! Two point one!' It was MacAlpine's turn to take up the head-shaking. 'Impossible. A margin like that? Impossible.'

'Ask the time-keepers. He did it twice.'

'Jesus!'

'You don't seem as pleased as you might, James.'

'Pleased. I'm bloody well terrified. Sure, sure, he's still the best driver in the world – except in actual competition when his nerve goes. But it wasn't driving skill that took him around in that time. It was Dutch courage. Sheer bloody suicidal Dutch courage.'

'I don't understand you.'

'He'd a half-bottle of scotch inside him, Alexis.'

Dunnet stared at him. He said at length, 'I don't believe it. I can't believe it. He may have driven like a bat out of hell but he also drove like an angel. Half a bottle of scotch? He'd have killed himself.'

'Perhaps it's as well there was no one else on the track at the time. He'd have killed them, maybe.'

'But – but a whole half-bottle!'

'Want to come and have a look in the cistern in his bathroom?'

'No, no. You think I'd ever question your word? It's just that I can't understand it.'

'Nor can I, nor can I. And where is our world champion at the moment?'

'Left the track. Says he's through for the day. Says he's got the pole position for tomorrow and if anyone takes it from him he'll just come back and take it away from them again. He's in an uppish sort of mood today, is our Johnny.'

'And he never used to talk that way. That's not uppishness, Alexis, it's sheer bloody euphoria dancing on clouds of seventy proof. God Almighty, do I have a problem or do I have a problem.'

'You have a problem, James.'

* * *

On the afternoon of that same Saturday MacAlpine, had he been in a certain rather shabby little side street in Monza, might well have had justification for thinking that his problems were being doubly or trebly compounded. Two highly undistinguished little cafés faced each other across the narrow street. They had in common the same peeling paint façade, hanging reed curtains, chequered cloth-covered sidewalk tables and bare, functional and splendidly uninspired interiors. And both of them, as was so common in cafés of this type, featured high-backed booths facing end-on to the street.

Sitting well back from the window in such a booth on the southern and shaded side of the street were Neubauer and Tracchia with untouched drinks in front of them. The drinks were untouched because neither man was interested in them. Their entire interest was concentrated upon the café opposite where, close up to the window and clearly in view, Harlow and Dunnet, glasses in their hands, could be seen engaged in what appeared to be earnest discussion across their booth table.

Neubauer said: 'Well, now that we've followed them here, Nikki, what do we do now? I mean, you can't lip-read, can you?'

'We wait and see? We play it by ear? I wish to God I could lip-read, Willi. And I'd also like to know why those two have suddenly become so friendly – though they hardly ever speak nowadays in public. And why did they have to come to a little back street like this to talk? We know that Harlow is up to something very funny indeed – the back of my neck still feels half-broken, I could hardly get my damned helmet on today. And if he and Dunnet are so thick then they're both up to the same funny thing. But Dunnet's only a journalist. What can a journalist and a has-been driver be up to?'

'Has-been? Did you see his times this morning?'

'Has-been I said and has-been I meant. You'll see – he'll crack tomorrow just as he's cracked in the last four GPs.'

'Yes. Another strange thing. Why is he so good in practice and such a failure in the races themselves?'

'No question. It's common knowledge that Harlow's pretty close to being an alcoholic – I'd say he already is one. All right, so he can drive one fast lap, maybe three. But in an eighty-lap Grand Prix – how can you expect an alco to have the stamina, the reactions, the nerve to last the pace? He'll crack.' He looked away from the other café and took a morose sip of his drink. 'God, what wouldn't I give to be sitting in the next booth to those two.'

Tracchia laid a hand on Neubauer's forearm. 'Maybe that won't be necessary, Willi. Maybe we've just found a pair of ears to do our listening for us. Look!'

Neubauer looked. With what appeared to be a considerable degree of stealth and secrecy Rory MacAlpine was edging his way into the booth next to the one occupied by Harlow and Dunnet. He was carrying a coloured drink in his hand. When he sat it was with his back to Harlow: physically, they couldn't have been more than a foot apart. Rory adopted a very upright posture, both his back and the back of his head pressed hard against the partition: he was, clearly, listening very intently indeed. He had about him the look of one who was planning a career either as a master spy or a double agent. Without question he had a rare talent for observing – and listening – without being observed.

Neubauer said: 'What do you think young MacAlpine is up to?'

'Here and now?' Tracchia spread his hands. 'Anything. The one thing that you can be sure of is that he intends no good to Harlow. I should think he is just trying to get anything he can on Harlow. Just anything. He's a determined young devil – and he hates Harlow. I must say I wouldn't care very much myself to be in his black books.'

'So we have an ally, Nikki, yes?'

'I see no reason why not. Let's think up a nice little story to tell him.' He peered across the street. 'Young Rory doesn't seem too pleased about something.'

Rory wasn't. His expression held mixed feelings of vexation, exasperation and perplexity: because of the high back of the booth and the background noise level created by the other patrons of the café, he could catch only snatches of the conversation from the next booth.

Matters weren't helped for Rory by the fact that Harlow and Dunnet were carrying on this conversation in very low tones indeed. Both of them had tall clear drinks in front of them, both drinks with ice and lemon in them: only one held gin. Dunnet looked consideringly at the tiny film cassette he was cradling in the palm of his hand then slipped it into a safe inside pocket.

'Photographs of code? You're sure?'

'Code for sure. Perhaps even along with some abstruse foreign language. I'm afraid I'm no expert on those matters.'

'No more than I am. But we have people who are experts. And the Coronado transporter. You're sure about that too?'

'No question.'

'So we've been nursing a viper to our own bosom – if that's the phrase I'm looking for.'

'It is a bit embarrassing, isn't it?'

'And no question about Henry having any finger in the pie?'

'Henry?' Harlow shook his head positively. 'My life on it.'

'Even though, as driver, he's the only person who's with the transporter on every trip it makes?'

'Even though.'

'And Henry will have to go?'

'What option do we have?'

'So. Exit Henry – temporarily, though he won't know it: he'll get his old job back. He'll be hurt, of course – but what's one brief hurt to 'thousands of life-long ones?'

'And if he refuses?'

'I'll have him kidnapped,' Dunnet said matter-of-factly. 'Or otherwise removed – painlessly, of course. But he'll go along. I've got the doctor's certificate already signed.'

'How about medical ethics?'

'The combination of £500 and a genuine certificate of an already existing heart murmur makes medical scruples vanish like a snowflake in the river.'

The two men finished their drinks, rose and left. So, after what he presumably regarded as being a suitably safe interval, did Rory. In the café opposite, Neubauer and Tracchia rose hurriedly, walked quickly after Rory and overtook him in half a minute. Rory looked his surprise.

Tracchia said confidentially: 'We want to talk to you, Rory. Can you keep a secret?'

Rory looked intrigued but he had a native caution which seldom abandoned him. 'What's the secret about?'

'You *are* a suspicious young person.'

'What's the secret about?'

'Johnny Harlow.'

'That's different.' Tracchia had Rory's instantaneous and co-operative attention. 'Of course I can keep a secret.'

Neubauer said: 'Well, then, never a whisper. Never one word or you'll ruin everything. You understand?'

'Of course.' He hadn't the faintest idea what Neubauer was talking about.

'You've heard of the GPDA?'

'Course. The Grand Prix Drivers' Association.'

'Right. Well, the GPDA has decided that for the safety of us all, drivers and spectators alike, Harlow must be removed from the Grand Prix roster. We want him taken off all the race-tracks in Europe. You know that he drinks?'

'Who doesn't?'

'He drinks so much that he's become the most dangerous driver in Europe.' Neubauer's voice was low-pitched, conspiratorial and totally convincing. 'Every other driver is scared to be on the same track as he is. None of us knows when he's going to be the next Jethou.'

'You – you mean – '

'He was drunk at the time. That's why a good man dies, Rory – because another man drinks half a bottle of scotch too many. Would you call that much different from being a murderer?'

'No, by God I wouldn't!'

'So the GPDA has asked Willi and myself to gather the evidence. About drinking, I mean. Especially before a big race. Will you help us?'

'You have to ask me?'

'We know, boy, we know.' Neubauer put his hand on Rory's shoulder, a gesture at once indicative of consolation and understanding. 'Mary is our girl, too. You saw Harlow and Mr Dunnet in that café just now. Did Harlow drink?'

'I didn't really see them. I was in the next booth. But I heard Mr Dunnet say something about gin and I saw the waiter bring two tall glasses with what looked like water in them.'

'Water!' Tracchia shook his head sadly. 'Anyway, that's more like it. Though I can't believe that Dunnet – well, who knows. Did you hear them talk about drink?'

'Mr Dunnet? Is there something wrong with him too?'

Tracchia said evasively, well aware that that was the surest way of arousing Rory's interest: 'I don't know anything about Mr Dunnet. About drink, now.'

'They spoke in very low voices. I caught something, not much. Not about drink. The only thing I heard was something about changed cassettes – film cassettes – or such-like, something Harlow had given to Mr Dunnet. Didn't make any kind of sense to me.'

Tracchia said: 'That hardly concerns us. But the rest, yes. Keep your eyes and ears open, will you?'

Rory, carefully concealing his new-found sense of self-importance, nodded man to man and walked away. Neubauer and Tracchia looked at each other with fury in their faces, a fury, clearly, that was not directed at each other.

Through tightly clenched teeth Tracchia said: 'The crafty bastard! He's switched cassettes on us. That was a dud we destroyed.'

On the evening of that same day Dunnet and Henry sat in a remote corner of the lobby in the Villa-Hotel Cessni. Dunnet wore his usual near-inscrutable expression. Henry looked somewhat stunned although it was clear that his native shrewdness was hard at work making a reassessment of an existing situation and a readjustment to a developing one. He tried hard not to look cunning. He said: 'You certainly do know how to lay it on the line, don't you, Mr Dunnet?' The tone of respectful admiration for a higher intellect was perfectly done. Dunnet remained totally unmoved.

'If by laying it on the line, Henry, you mean putting it as briefly and clearly as possible, then, yes, I have laid it on the line. Yes or no?'

'Jesus, Mr Dunnet, you don't give a man much time to think, do you?'

Dunnet said patiently: 'This hardly calls for thought, Henry. A simple yes or no. Take it or leave it.'

Henry kept his cunning look under wraps. 'And if I leave it?'

'We'll cross that bridge when we come to it.'

Henry looked distinctly uneasy. 'I don't know if I like the sound of that, Mr Dunnet.'

'How does it sound to you, Henry?'

'I mean, well, you aren't blackmailing me or threatening me or something like that?'

Dunnet had the air of a man counting up to ten. 'You make me say it, Henry. You're talking rubbish. How can one blackmail a man who leads the spotless life you do? You do lead a spotless life, don't you, Henry? And *why* should I threaten you? *How* could I threaten you?' He made a long pause. 'Yes or no?'

Henry sighed in defeat. 'Damn it all, yes. I've got nothing to lose. For £5,000 and a job in our Marseilles garage I'd sell my own grandmother down the river – God rest her soul.'

'That wouldn't be necessary even if it were possible. Just total silence that's all. Here's a health certificate from a local doctor. It's to say you have an advanced cardiac condition and are no longer fit for heavy work such as, say, driving a transporter.'

'I haven't been feeling at all well lately and that's a fact.'

Dunnet permitted himself the faintest of smiles. 'I thought you might have been feeling that way.'

'Does Mr MacAlpine know about this?'

'He will when you tell him. Just wave that paper.'

'You think he'll wear it?'

'If you mean accept it, yes. He'll have no option.'

'May I ask the reason for all this?'

'No. You're getting paid £5,000 not to ask questions. Or talk. Ever.'

'You're a very funny journalist, Mr Dunnet.'

'Very.'

'I'm told you were an accountant in what they call the City. Why did you give it up?'

'Emphysema. My lungs, Henry, my lungs.'

'Something like my cardiac condition?'

'In these days of stress and strain, Henry, perfect health is a blessing that is granted to very few of us. And now you'd better go and see Mr MacAlpine.'

Henry left. Dunnet wrote a brief note, addressed a stout buff envelope, marked it EXPRESS and URGENT in the top left corner, inserted the note and microfilm and left. As he passed out into the corridor he failed to notice that the door of the room next to his was slightly ajar: consequently, he also failed to observe a single eye peering out through this narrow gap in the doorway.

The eye belonged to Tracchia. He closed the door, moved out on to his balcony and waved an arm in signal. In the distance, far beyond the forecourt of the hotel, an indistinct figure raised an arm in acknowledgment. Tracchia hurried downstairs and located Neubauer. Together they moved towards the bar and sat there, ordering soft drinks. At least a score of people saw and recognized them for Neubauer and Tracchia were scarcely less well known that Harlow himself. But Tracchia was not a man to establish an alibi by halves.

He said to the barman: 'I'm expecting a call from Milan at five o'clock. What time do you have?'

'Exactly five, Mr Tracchia.'

'Let the desk know I'm here.'

The direct route to the Post Office lay through a narrow alleyway lined with mews-type houses and alternate garages on both sides. The road was almost deserted, a fact that Dunnet attributed to its being a Saturday afternoon. In all its brief length of less than two hundred yards there was only an overalled figure working over the engine of his car outside the opened door of a garage. In a fashion more French than Italian he wore a navy beret down to his eyes and the rest of his face was so streaked with oil and grease as to be virtually unrecognizable. He wouldn't, Dunnet thought inconsequentially, have been tolerated for five seconds on the Coronado racing team. But, then, working on a Coronado and on a battered old Fiat 600 called for different standards of approach.

As Dunnet passed the Fiat the mechanic abruptly straightened. Dunnet politely side-stepped to avoid him but as he did so the mechanic, one leg braced against the side of the car to lend additional leverage for a take-off thrust, flung his entire bodily weight against him. Completely off-balance and already falling, Dunnet staggered through the opened garage doorway. His already headlong process towards the ground was rapidly and violently accelerated by two very large and very powerful stocking-masked figures who clearly held no brief for the more gentle arts of persuasion. The garage door closed behind him.

Rory was absorbed in a lurid comic magazine and Tracchia and Neubauer, alibis safely established, were still at the bar when Dunnet entered the hotel. It was an entry that attracted the immediate attention of everyone in the foyer for it was an entry that would have attracted such attention anywhere. Dunnet didn't walk in, he staggered in like a drunken man and even then would have fallen were it not for the fact that he was supported by a policeman on either side of him. He was bleeding badly from nose and mouth, had a rapidly closing right eye, an unpleasant gash above it and, generally, a badly bruised face. Tracchia, Neubauer, Rory and the receptionist reached him at almost the same moment.

The shock in Tracchia's voice marched perfectly with the expression on his face. He said: 'God in heaven, Mr Dunnet, what happened to you?'

Dunnet tried to smile, winced and thought better of it. He said in a slurred voice: 'I rather think I was set upon.'

Neubauer said: 'But who did – I mean where – why, Mr Dunnet, why?'

One of the policemen held up his hand and turned to the receptionist. 'Please. At once. A doctor.'

'In one minute. Less. We have seven staying here. She turned to Tracchia. 'You know Mr Dunnet's room, Mr Tracchia. If you and Mr Neubauer would be so kind as to show the officers – '

'No need. Mr Neubauer and I will take him up.'

The policeman said: 'I'm sorry. We will require a statement from – '

He halted as most people did when they were on the receiving end of Tracchia's most intimidating scowl. He said: 'Leave your station number with this young lady. You will be called when the doctor gives Mr Dunnet permission to talk. Not before. Meantime, he must get to bed immediately. Do you understand?'

They understood, nodded and left without another word. Tracchia and Neubauer, followed by a Rory whose puzzlement was matched only by his apprehension, took Dunnet to his room and were in the process of putting him to bed when a doctor arrived. He was young, Italian, clearly highly efficient and extremely polite when he asked them to leave the room.

In the corridor Rory said: 'Why would anyone do that to Mr Dunnet?'

'Who knows?' Tracchia said. 'Robbers, thieves, people who would sooner rob and half-kill than do an honest day's work.' He flicked a glance at Neubauer, one that Rory was not intended to miss. 'There are lots of unpleasant people in the world, Rory. Let's leave it to the police, shall we?'

'You mean that you're not going to bother – '

'We're drivers, my boy,' Neubauer said. 'We're not detectives.'

'I'm not a boy! I'll soon be seventeen. And I'm not a fool.' Rory brought his anger under control and looked at them speculatively. 'There's something very fishy, very funny going on. I'll bet Harlow is mixed up in this somewhere.'

'Harlow?' Tracchia raised an amused eyebrow in a fashion that was little to Rory's liking. 'Come off it, Rory. *You* were the person who overheard Harlow and Dunnet having their confidential little *tête-à-tête*.'

'Aha! That's just the point. I *didn't* overhear what they said. I just heard their voices, not what they said. They could have been saying anything. Maybe Harlow was threatening him.' Rory paused to consider this fresh and intriguing prospect and conviction burgeoned on the instant. 'Of course that was what it was. Harlow was threatening him because Dunnet was either double-crossing or blackmailing him.'

Tracchia said kindly: 'Rory, you really must give up reading those horror comics of yours. Even if Dunnet were double-crossing or blackmailing Harlow, how would beating up Dunnet help in any way? He's still around, isn't he? He can still carry on this double-crossing or blackmailing of yours. I'm afraid you'll have to come up with a better one than that, Rory.'

Rory said slowly: 'Maybe I can. Dunnet did say he was beaten up in that narrow alleyway leading towards the main street. Do you know what lies at the far end of the alleyway? The Post Office. Maybe Dunnet was going down there to dispose of some evidence he had on Harlow. Maybe he thought it was too dangerous to carry that evidence around with him any more. So Harlow made good and sure that Dunnet never got the chance to post it.'

Neubauer looked at Tracchia then back at Rory. He wasn't smiling any more. He said: 'What kind of evidence, Rory?'

'How should I know?' Rory's irritation was marked. 'I've been doing all the thinking up till now. How about you two trying to do a little thinking for once?'

'We might just at that.' Tracchia, like Neubauer, was now suddenly serious and thoughtful. 'Now don't go talking around about this, lad. Apart from the fact that we haven't a single shred of proof, there's such a thing as the law of libel.'

'I've told you once,' Rory said with some acerbity, 'I'm not a fool. Besides, it wouldn't look too good for you two if it was known that you were trying to put the finger on Johnny Harlow.'

'That you can say again,' Tracchia said. 'Bad news travels fast. Here comes Mr MacAlpine.'

MacAlpine arrived at the head of the stairs, his face, much thinner now and far more deeply lined than it had been two months previously, was grim and tight with anger. He said: 'This is true? I mean about Dunnet?'

Tracchia said: 'I'm afraid so. Some person or persons have given him a pretty thorough going over.'

'In God's name, why?'

'Robbery, it looks like.'

'Robbery! In broad daylight. Jesus, the sweet joys of civilization. When did this happen?'

'Couldn't have been much more than ten minutes ago. Willi and I were at the bar when he went out. It was exactly five o'clock because I happened to be checking a phone call with the barman at the time. We were at the bar when he came back and when he came back I checked my watch – thought it might be useful for the police to know. It was exactly twelve minutes past five. He couldn't have got very far in that time.'

'Where is he now?'

'There. In his room.'

'Then why are you three – '

'Doctor's in there with him. He threw us out.'

'He will not,' MacAlpine predicted with certainty, 'throw me out.'

Nor did he. Five minutes later it was the doctor who was the first to emerge followed in another five by MacAlpine, his face at once thunderous and deeply worried. He went straight to his own room.

Tracchia, Neubauer and Rory were sitting by a wall table in the foyer when Harlow entered. If he saw them he paid no heed but walked straight across the length of the foyer to the stairs. He smiled faintly once or twice in response to tentative approaches and deferential smiles of greeting, but otherwise his face remained its normal impassive self.

Neubauer said: 'Well, you must admit that our Johnny doesn't look all that concerned about life.'

'You bet he doesn't.' Rory could not have been accused of snarling, because he hadn't yet mastered the art, but he was obviously getting close. 'I'll bet he's not very concerned about death either. I'll bet if it was his own grandmother he'd – '

'Rory.' Tracchia held up a restraining hand. 'You're letting your imagination run wild. The Grand Prix Drivers' Association is a very respectable body of men. We have what people call a good public image and we don't want to spoil it. Sure, we like to have you on our side: but wild talk like this can only damage everyone concerned.'

Rory scowled at each man in turn, rose and walked stiffly away. Neubauer said, almost sadly: 'I'm afraid, Nikki, that our young firebrand there is shortly about to experience some of the most painful moments of his life.'

'It'll do him no harm,' Tracchia said. 'And it certainly won't do us any either.'

Neubauer's prophecy was confirmed in remarkably short order.

* * *

Harlow closed the door behind him and looked down at the prostrate figure of Dunnet who, although he had been duly and efficiently doctored, had a face that looked as if it had emerged from a major road accident within the past few minutes. Allowing for the areas covered by bruises and a variety of plasters, there was, in all conscience, little enough of his face to be seen, just a nose double its usual size, a completely-closed rainbow-coloured right eye and stitches on the forehead and upper lip, but sufficient to lend credence to his recent life and hard times. Harlow clucked his tongue in the usual sympathetic if rather perfunctory fashion, took two silent steps towards the door and jerked it open. Rory literally fell into the room and measured his length on the splendid marble tiles of the Villa-Hotel Cessni.

Wordlessly, Harlow bent over him, wound his fingers in Rory's thick black curling hair and hauled him to his feet. Rory had no words either, just a piercing heartfelt scream of agony. Still without speaking, Harlow transferred his grip to Rory's ear, marched him along the corridor to MacAlpine's room, knocked and went inside, dragging Rory with him: tears of pain rolled down the unhappy Rory's face. MacAlpine, lying on top of his bed, propped himself up on one elbow: his outrage that his only son should be so cruelly mishandled was clearly outweighed by the fact that it was Harlow who was doing the mishandling.

Harlow said: 'I know I'm not very much in the grace and favour line with Coronado at the moment. I also know he is your son. But the next time I find this spying young tramp eavesdropping outside the door of a room I'm in I'll well and truly clobber him.'

MacAlpine looked at Harlow, then at Rory, then back to Harlow. 'I can't believe it. I won't believe it.' The voice was flat and singularly lacking in conviction.

'I don't care whether you believe me or not.' Harlow's anger had gone, he'd slipped on his old mask of indifference. 'But I know you would believe Alexis Dunnet. Go and ask him. I was with him in his room when I opened the door a bit unexpectedly for our young friend here. He had been leaning so heavily against it that he fell flat to the floor. I helped him up. By his hair. That's why there's tears in his eyes.'

MacAlpine looked at Rory in a less than paternal fashion. 'Is this true?'

Rory wiped his sleeve across his eyes, concentrated sullenly on the examination of the toes of his shoes and prudently said nothing.

'Leave him to me, Johnny.' MacAlpine didn't look particularly angry or upset, just very very tired. 'My apologies if I seemed to doubt you – I didn't.'

Harlow nodded, left, returned to Dunnet's room, closed and locked the door then, as Dunnet watched in silence, proceeded to search the room thoroughly. A few minutes later, apparently still not satisfied, he moved into the adjacent bathroom, turned a tap and the shower on to maximum then went out, leaving the door wide open behind him. It is difficult for even the most sensitive microphone to pick up with any degree of clarity the sound of human voices against a background of running water.

Without any by-your-leave, he searched through the outer clothing that Dunnet had been wearing. He replaced the clothing and looked at Dunnet's torn shirt and the white band that a wrist watch had left on a sun-tanned wrist.

'Has it occurred to you, Alexis,' Harlow said, 'that some of your activities are causing displeasure in certain quarters and that they are trying to discourage you?'

'Funny. Bloody funny.' Dunnet's voice was, understandably, so thick and slurred that in his case the use of any anti-microphone devices was almost wholly superfluous. 'Why didn't they discourage me permanently?'

'Only a fool kills unnecessarily. We are not up against fools. However, who knows, one day? Well, now. Wallet, loose change, watch, cuff-links, even your half-dozen fountain pens and car keys – all gone. Looks like a pretty professional roll job, doesn't it?'

'The hell with that.' Dunnet spat blood into a handful of tissue. 'What matters is that the cassette is gone.'

Harlow hesitated then cleared his throat in a diffident fashion.

'Well, let's say that *a* cassette is missing.'

The only really viable feature in Dunnet's face was his unblemished right eye: this, after a momentary puzzlement, he used most effectively to glower at Harlow with the maximum of suspicion.

'What the hell do you mean?'

Harlow gazed into the middle distance.

'Well, Alexis, I do feel a little bit apologetic about this, but the cassette that matters is in the hotel safe. The one our friends now have – the one I gave to you – was a plant.'

Dunnet, with what little could be seen of his sadly battered face slowly darkening in anger, tried to sit up: gently but firmly Harlow pushed him down again.

Harlow said: 'Now, now, Alexis, don't do yourself an injury. Another one, I mean. They were on to me and I had to put myself in the clear or I was finished – although God knows I never expected them to do this to you.' He paused. 'I'm in the clear now.'

'You'd better be sure of that, my boy.' Dunnet had subsided but his anger hadn't.

'I'm sure. When they develop that film spool they'll find it contains micro photos – about a hundred – of line drawings of a prototype gas turbine engine. They'll conclude I'm as much a criminal as they are, but as my business is industrial espionage, there can be no possible conflict of interests. They'll lose interest in me.'

Dunnet looked at him balefully. 'Clever bastard, aren't you?'

'Yes, I am, rather.' He went to the door, opened it and turned round. 'Especially, it seems, when it is at other people's expense.'

CHAPTER SEVEN

In the Coronado pits on the following afternoon a heavily panting MacAlpine and a still sadly battered Dunnet argued in low and urgent tones. The faces of both men were marked with worry.

MacAlpine made no attempt to conceal the savagery he felt inside him. He said: 'But the bottle's empty, man. Drained to the last drop. I've just checked. Jesus, I can't just let him go out there and kill another man.'

'If you stop him you'll have to explain why to the press. It'll be a sensation, the international sporting scandal of the last decade. It'll kill Johnny. Professionally, I mean.'

'Better have him killed professionally than have him kill another driver for real.'

Dunnet said: 'Give him two laps. If he's in the lead, then let him go. He can't kill anyone in that position. If not, flag him in. We'll cook up something for the press. Anyway, remember what he did yesterday with the same skinful inside him?'

'Yesterday he was lucky. Today – '

'Today it's too late.'

Even at a distance of several hundred feet the sound of twenty-four Grand Prix racing engines accelerating away from the starting grid was startling, almost shattering, both in its unexpectedness and ear-cringing fury of sound. MacAlpine and Dunnet looked at each other and shrugged simultaneously. There seemed to be no other comment or reaction to meet the case.

The first driver past the pits, already pulling fractionally clear of Nicolo Tracchia, was Harlow in his lime-green Coronado. MacAlpine turned to Dunnet and said heavily: 'One swallow does not make a summer.'

Eight laps later MacAlpine was beginning to question his ornithological expertise. He was looking slightly dazed while Dunnet was indulging in considerable eyebrow-lifting, Jacobson's expression was not one indicative of any marked internal pleasure while Rory was positively scowling although manfully trying not to. Only Mary expressed her true emotion and that without inhibition. She looked positively radiant.

'Three lap records gone,' she said incredulously. 'Three lap records in eight laps.'

By the end of the ninth lap the emotions of those in the Coronado pits, as registered by their facial expressions, had radically altered. Jacobson and Rory were, with difficulty, refraining from looking cheerful. Mary was chewing anxiously on her pencil. MacAlpine looked thunderous but the thunder was overlaid by deep anxiety.

'Forty seconds overdue!' he said. 'Forty seconds! All the field's gone past and he's not even in sight. What in God's name could have happened to him?'

Dunnet said: 'Shall I phone the track-marshals' checkpoints?'

MacAlpine nodded and Dunnet began to make calls. The first two yielded no information and he was about to make a third when Harlow's Coronado appeared and drew into the pits. The engine note of the Coronado sounded perfectly healthy in every way, which was more than could be said for Harlow when he had climbed out of his car and removed his helmet and goggles. His eyes were glazed, and bloodshot. He looked at them for a moment then spread his hands: the tremor in them was unmistakable.

'Sorry. Had to pull up about a mile out. Double vision. Could hardly see where I was going. Come to that, I still can't.'

'Get changed.' The bleak harshness in MacAlpine's voice startled the listeners. 'I'm taking you to hospital.'

Harlow hesitated, made as if to speak, shrugged, turned and walked away. Dunnet said in a low voice: 'You're not taking him to the course doctor?'

'I'm taking him to see a friend of mine. An optometrist of note but many other things besides. All I want him to do is a little job for me, a job I couldn't get done in privacy and secrecy on the track.'

Dunnet said quietly, almost sadly: 'A blood sample?'

'Just one positive blood sample.'

'And that will be the end of the road for Grand Prix's superstar?'

'The end of the road.'

For a person who might well have good reason for believing he had reached the end of his professional career Harlow, as he sat relaxed in his chair in a hospital corridor, seemed singularly unperturbed. Most unusually for him he was smoking a cigarette, the hand holding the cigarette as steady as if it had been carved from marble. Harlow gazed thoughtfully at the door at the far end of the corridor.

Behind that door MacAlpine, his face registering a combination of disbelief and consternation, looked at the man seated across the desk from him, a benign and elderly bearded doctor in shirt sleeves.

MacAlpine said: 'Impossible. Quite impossible. You mean to tell me there is *no* alcohol in his blood?'

'Impossible or not, I mean what I say. An experienced colleague has just carried out a double-check. He has no more alcohol in his blood than you would find in that of a life-long abstainer.'

MacAlpine shook his head. 'Impossible,' he repeated. 'Look, Professor, I have proof – '

'To us long-suffering doctors nothing is impossible. The speed with which different individuals metabolize alcohol varies beyond belief. With an obviously extremely fit young man like your friend outside – '

'But his eyes! You saw his eyes. Bleary, bloodshot – '

'There could be half a dozen reasons for that.'

'And the double vision?'

'His eyes seem normal enough. How well he is seeing it's hard to say yet. There exists always the possibility that the eyes themselves are sound enough but that some damage may have been done to an optical nerve.' The doctor stood up. 'A spot check is not enough. I'd need a series of tests, a battery of tests. Unfortunately, not now – I'm already overdue at the theatre. Could he come along about seven this evening?'

MacAlpine said he could, expressed his thanks and left. As he approached Harlow, he looked at the cigarette in his hand, then at Harlow, then back at the cigarette but said nothing. Still in silence, the two men left the hospital, got into MacAlpine's Aston and drove back in the direction of Monza.

Harlow broke the silence. He said mildly: 'As the principal concerned, don't you think you should tell me what the doctor said?'

MacAlpine said shortly: 'He's not sure. He wants to carry out a series of tests. The first is at seven o'clock tonight.'

Still mildly, Harlow said: 'I hardly think that will be necessary.'

MacAlpine glanced at him in brief speculation. 'And what's that meant to mean?'

'There's a lay-by half a kilometre ahead. Pull in, please. There's something I want to say.'

At seven o'clock that evening, the hour when Harlow was supposed to be in hospital, Dunnet sat in MacAlpine's hotel room. The atmosphere was funereal. Both men had large glasses of scotch in their hands.

Dunnet said: 'Jesus! Just like that? He said his nerve was gone, he knew he was finished and could he break his contract?'

'Just like that. No more beating about the bush, he said. No more kidding – especially kidding himself. God knows what it cost the poor devil to say so.'

'And the scotch?'

MacAlpine sampled his own and sighed heavily, more in sadness than weariness. 'Quite humorous about it, really. Says he detests the damned stuff and is thankful for a reason never to touch it again.'

It was Dunnet's turn to have recourse to his scotch. 'And what's going to happen to your poor devil now? Mind you, James, I'm not overlooking what this has cost you – you've lost the best driver in the world. But right now I'm more concerned about Johnny.'

'Me, too. But what to do? What to do?'

The man who was the subject of all this concern was displaying a remarkable amount of unconcern. For a man who was the central figure in the greatest fall from grace in the history of motor racing, Johnny Harlow seemed most extraordinarily cheerful. As he adjusted his tie before the mirror in his room he whistled, albeit slightly tunelessly, to himself, breaking off occasionally to smile at some private thought. He shrugged into his jacket, left his room, went down to the lobby, took an orangeade from the bar and sat down at a nearby table. Before he was even able to sip his drink Mary came and sat beside him. She took one of his hands in both of hers.

'Johnny!' she said. 'Oh, Johnny!'

'Harlow gazed at her with sorrowful eyes.

She went on: 'Daddy just told me. Oh, Johnny, what are we going to do?'

'We?'

She gazed at him for long seconds without speaking, looked away and said: 'To lose my two best friends in one day.' There were no tears in her eyes but there were tears in her voice.

'Your two – what do you mean?'

'I thought you knew.' Now the tears were trickling down her cheeks. 'Henry's got bad heart trouble. He has to go.'

'Henry? Dear, oh dear, oh dear.' Harlow squeezed her hands and gazed off into the middle distance. 'Poor old Henry. I wonder what will happen to him?'

'Oh, that's all right.' She sniffed. 'Daddy's keeping him on in Marseilles.'

'Ah. Then it's probably all for the best – Henry was getting past it anyway.'

Harlow remained thoughtful for some seconds, apparently lost in deep thought, then clasped Mary's hands with his free one. He said: 'Mary, I love you. Hang on, will you? Back in a couple of minutes.'

One minute later Harlow was in MacAlpine's room. Dunnet was there and he had the appearance of a man who was with difficulty keeping his anger under control. MacAlpine was clearly highly distressed. He shook his head many times.

He said: 'Not at any price. Not under any circumstances. No, no, no. It's just not on. One day the world champion, the next trundling a lumbering transporter all over the place. Why, man, you'd be the laughing stock of Europe.'

'Maybe.' Harlow's voice was quiet, without bitterness. 'But not half as much a laughing stock as I'd be if people knew the real reason for my retiral, Mr MacAlpine.'

'Mr MacAlpine? Mr MacAlpine? I'm always James to you, my boy. Always have been.'

'Not any more, sir. You could explain about my so-called double vision, say that I've been retained as a specialist adviser. What more natural? Besides, you *do* need a transporter driver.'

MacAlpine shook his head in slow and complete finality. 'Johnny Harlow will never drive any transporter of mine and that's the end of it.'

MacAlpine covered his face with his hands. Harlow looked at Dunnet who jerked his head towards the door. Harlow nodded and left the room.

Dunnet let some seconds pass in silence, then he said, picking his words carefully and without emotion: 'And that's the end of me. I'll say goodbye to you, then, James MacAlpine. I've enjoyed every minute of my assignment. Except for the last minute.'

MacAlpine removed his hands, slowly lifted his head and stared at Dunnet in wonderment. He said: 'What on earth do you mean?'

'I mean this. Isn't it obvious? I value my health too much to stay around and feel sick every time I think of what you've done. That boy lives for motor racing, it's the only thing he knows and now he has no place left in the world to go. And I would remind you, James MacAlpine, that in the space of four short years the Coronado has been hauled up from the depths of near obscurity and made into the most successful and respected Grand Prix racing car in the world through one thing and one thing only – the incomparable driving genius of that boy to whom you have just shown the door. Not you, James, not you. Johnny Harlow made Coronado. But you can't afford to be associated with failure, he's no use to you any more so you drop him into the discard. I hope you sleep well tonight, Mr MacAlpine. You should do. You have every reason to be proud of yourself.'

Dunnet turned to leave. MacAlpine, with tears in his eyes, spoke softly. 'Alexis.'

Dunnet turned.

MacAlpine said: 'If you ever speak to me like that again I'll break your blasted neck. I'm tired, I'm dead tired, and I want to sleep before dinner. Go tell him he can have any bloody job he likes on the Coronado – mine, if he so cares.'

Dunnet said: 'I've been bloody rude. Please accept my apologies. And thank you very much, James.'

MacAlpine smiled faintly. 'Not Mr MacAlpine?'

'I said "Thank you, James".'

Both men smiled at each other. Dunnet left, closing the door with a quiet hand, went down in to the lobby where Harlow and Mary were seated side by side, untouched drinks before them. The aura of profound despondency that overhung their table was almost palpable. Dunnet picked up a drink from the bar, joined Harlow and Mary, smiled broadly, lifted his glass and said: 'Cheers. Here's to the fastest transporter driver in Europe.'

Harlow left his drink untouched. He said: 'Alexis, I'm in one of my less humorous moods this evening.'

Dunnet said cheerfully: 'Mr James MacAlpine has had a sudden and complete change of mind and heart. His final words were "Go and tell him he can have any blasted job he likes on the Coronado – mine, if he so cares."' Harlow shook his head. Dunnet went on: 'God's sake, Johnny, I'm not having you on.'

Harlow shook his head again. 'I'm not doubting you, Alexis. I'm just flabbergasted. How on earth did you manage – well, perhaps it's just as well you don't tell me.' He smiled faintly. 'I don't think I really want Mr MacAlpine's job.'

'Oh, Johnny!' There were tears in her eyes but not tears of sorrow, not in that radiant face. She rose, flung her arms around his neck and kissed him on the cheek. Harlow, though slightly startled, was not noticeably embarrassed.

'That's my girl,' Dunnet said approvingly. 'A last long farewell to the fastest lorry driver in Europe.'

She stared at him. 'What on earth do you mean?'

'The transporter leaves for Marseilles tonight. Someone has to drive it there. This is a job usually reserved for the transporter driver.'

Harlow said: 'My God! I'd rather overlooked that part of it. Now?'

'As ever was. There appears to be a considerable degree of urgency. I think you'd better see James now.'

Harlow nodded, rose and left for his room where he changed into dark trousers, navy roll-neck sweater and leather jacket. He went to see MacAlpine and found him stretched out on his bed looking ill and pale and little short of positively haggard.

MacAlpine said: 'I have to admit, Johnny, that the reason for my decision is based largely on self-interest. Tweedledum and Tweedledee, good mechanics though they are, couldn't drive a wheelbarrow. Jacobson has already left for Marseilles to make loading arrangements for the morning. It's asking a lot, I know, but I must have number four, the new X car and the spare engine at the Vignolles test track by noon tomorrow – we have the track for two days only. A lot of driving, I know, and you'll have only a few hours' sleep, if that. You'll have to start loading in Marseilles by 6 a.m.'

'Fine. Now what shall I do with my own car?'

'Ah! The only transporter driver in Europe with his own Ferrari. Alexis will take my Aston while I, personally, will drive your rusty old bucket of bolts to Vignolles tomorrow. Then you'll have to take it to our Marseilles garage and leave it there. For keeps, I'm afraid.'

'I understand, Mr MacAlpine.'

'Mr MacAlpine, Mr MacAlpine. Are you sure this is what you want to do, Johnny?'

'Never surer, sir.'

Harlow went down to the lounge to find that Mary and Dunnet were no longer there. He went upstairs again, found Dunnet in his room and asked: 'Where's Mary?'

'Gone for a walk.'

'Bloody chilly evening to go for a walk.'

'I don't think she's in any condition to feel the cold,' Dunnet said drily. 'Euphoria, I believe they call it. Seen the old boy?'

'Yes. The old boy, as you call him, really is becoming an old boy. He's put on five years in the last six months.'

'More like ten years. Understandable with his wife vanishing just like that. Maybe if you'd lost someone to whom you've been married for twenty-five years – '

'He's lost more than that.'

'What's that supposed to mean?'

'I don't even know myself. His nerve, his self-confidence, his drive, his will to fight and win.' Harlow smiled. 'Some time this week we'll give him those lost ten years back again.'

'You're the most incredibly arrogant, self-confident bastard I've ever known,' Dunnet said admiringly. When Harlow made no reply, he shrugged and sighed. 'Well, to be a world champion I suppose you have to have some little belief in yourself. And now what?'

'Off. On my way out I'll pick up from the hotel safe this little bauble that I'm going to deliver to our friend in the rue St Pierre – seems a damned sight safer than trying to walk to the Post Office. How about having a drink in the bar and seeing if anyone's interested in me?'

'Why should they be? They have the right cassette – or think they have, which amounts to the same thing.'

'That's as maybe. But it's just possible that the ungodly might change their minds when they see me taking this envelope from the hotel safe, rip it open, throw the envelope away, examine the cassette and stick it in my pocket. They know they've been fooled once. You can bet your life that they'll be more than prepared to believe that they've been fooled twice.'

For long seconds Dunnet stared at Harlow in total disbelief. When he spoke, his voice was a whisper. He said: 'This isn't just asking for trouble. This is ordering your own pine box.'

'Only the best of oak for world champions. With gold-plated handles. Come on.'

They went down the stairs together. Dunnet turned off towards the bar while Harlow went to the desk. As Dunnet's eyes roved round the lobby, Harlow asked for and received his envelope, opened it, extracted the cassette and examined it carefully before putting it in an inside pocket of his leather jacket. As he turned away from the desk, Dunnet wandered up almost casually and said in a quiet voice. 'Tracchia. His eyes almost popped out of his head. He almost ran to the nearest phone booth.'

Harlow nodded, said nothing, passed through the swing doors, then halted as his way was barred by a leather-coated figure. He said: 'What are you doing here, Mary? It's bitterly cold.'

'I just wanted to say goodbye, that's all.'

'You could have said goodbye inside.'

'I'm a very private person.'

'Besides, you'll be seeing me again tomorrow. In Vignolles.'

'Will I, Johnny? Will I?'

'Tsk! Tsk! Someone else who doesn't believe I can drive.'

'Don't try to be funny, Johnny, because I'm not feeling that way. I'm feeling sick. I've this awful feeling that something dreadful is going to happen. To you.'

Harlow said lightly: 'It's this half-Highland blood of yours. Fey is what they call it. Having the second sight. If it's any consolation to you the second-sighters have an almost perfect 100 per cent record of failure.'

'Don't laugh at me, Johnny.' There were tears in her voice.

He put an arm round her shoulders.

'Laugh at you? With you, yes. At you, never.'

'Come back to me, Johnny.'

'I'll always come back to you, Mary.'

'What? What did vou say, Johnny?'

'A slip of the tongue.' He squeezed her shoulders, pecked her briskly on the cheek and strode off into the gathering darkness.

CHAPTER EIGHT

The giant Coronado transporter, its vast silhouette outlined by at least a score of lights on the sides and back, not to mention its four powerful headlamps, rumbled through the darkness and along the almost wholly deserted roads at a speed which would not have found very much favour with the Italian police speed patrols, had there been any such around that night which, fortunately, there weren't.

Harlow had elected to take the autostrada across to Turin then turned south to Cuneo and was now approaching the Col de Tende, that fearsome mountain pass with the tunnel at the top which marks the boundary between Italy and France. Even in an ordinary car, in daylight and in good dry driving conditions, it calls for the closest of care and attention: the steepness of the ascent and descent and the seemingly endless series of murderous hairpin bends on both sides of the tunnel make it as dangerous and difficult a pass as any in Europe. But to drive a huge transporter, at the limit of its adhesion and road-holding in rain that was now beginning to fall quite heavily, was an experience that was hazardous to a degree.

For some, it was plainly not only hazardous but harrowing to a degree. The red-haired twin mechanics, one curled up in the bucket seat beside Harlow, the other stretched out on the narrow bunk behind the front seats, though quite exhausted were clearly never more wide awake in their lives. Not to put too fine a point on it, they were frankly terrified, either staring in horror at each other or closing their eyes as they slid and swayed wildly on each successive hairpin bend. And if they did leave the road it wouldn't be just to bump across the surrounding terrain: it would be to fall a very long way indeed and their chances of survival were non-existent. The twins were beginning to realize why old Henry had never made it as a Grand Prix driver.

If Harlow was aware of the very considerable inner turmoil he was causing, he gave no signs of it. His entire being was concentrated on his driving and on scanning the road two, even three hairpin bends ahead. Tracchia and, by now, Tracchia's associates knew that he was carrying the cassette and that they intended to separate him from that cassette Harlow did not for a moment doubt. When and where they would make their attempt was a matter for complete conjecture. Crawling round the hairpins leading to the top of the Col de Tende made them the perfect target for an ambush. Whoever his adversaries were, Harlow was convinced they were based in Marseilles. It was unlikely that they would care to take the risk of running foul of the Italian law. He was certain that he hadn't been trailed from Monza. The chances were that they didn't even know what route he was taking. They might wait until he was much nearer their home base or even arrived at it. On the other hand they might be considering the possibility that he was getting rid of the cassette en route. Speculation seemed not only unrewarding but useless. He put the wide variety of possibilities out of his mind and concentrated on his driving while still keeping every sense alert for danger. As it was they made the top of the Col without incident, passed through the Italian and French Customs and started on the wickedly winding descent on the other side.

When he came to La Giandola, he hesitated briefly. He could take the road to Ventimiglia thus taking advantage of the new autoroutes westwards along the Riviera or take the shorter but more winding direct route to Nice. He took into account that the Ventimiglia route would entail encountering the Italian and French Customs not once but twice again and decided on the direct route.

He made Nice without incident, followed the autoroute past Cannes, reached Toulon and took the N8 to Marseilles. It was about twenty miles out of Cannes, near the village of Beausset, that it happened.

As they rounded a bend they could see, about a quarter of a mile ahead, four lights, two stationary, two moving. The two moving lights were red and obviously hand-held, for they swung steadily through arcs of about ninety degrees.

There was an abrupt change in the engine note as Harlow dropped a gear. The sound brought the dozing twins to something like near wakefulness just in time to identify, a bare second after Harlow, the legends on the two stationary lights, red and blue and flashing alternately: one said STOP, the other POLICE. There were at least five men behind the lights, two of them standing in the middle of the road.

Harlow was hunched far forward over the wheel, his eyes narrowed until even the pupils seemed in danger of disappearing. He made an abrupt decision, arm and leg moved in swift and perfect unison, and again the engine note changed as the big diesel dropped another gear. Ahead, the two moving red lamps stopped swinging. It must have been evident to those wielding them that the transporter was slowing to a halt.

Fifty yards distant from the road-block Harlow stamped the accelerator pedal flat to the floor. The transporter, designedly, had been in the correct gear to pick up maximum acceleration and it was in that gear that Harlow held it, the engine revolutions climbing as the distance between the transporter and the flashing lights ahead steadily and rapidly decreased. The two men with the red lights moved rapidly apart: it had dawned on them, and a very rude awakening it must have been, that the transporter had no intention of stopping.

Inside the cab the faces of Tweedledum and Tweedledee registered identical expressions of horrified and incredulous apprehension. Harlow's face registered no expression at all as he watched the shadowy figures who had been standing so confidently in the middle of the road fling themselves to safety towards either verge. Above the still mounting roar of the diesel could be heard the sound of the splintering of glass and the screeching of buckling metal as the transporter over-ran the pedestal-mounted flashing lights in the middle of the road. Twenty yards farther on there came a series of heavy thuds from the rear of the transporter, a drumming sound that continued for another thirty or forty yards until Harlow swung the swaying transporter round a forty-five turn in the road. Harlow changed up once and then again into top gear. He appeared to be quite unconcerned which was considerably more than could be said for the twins.

Tweedledum said in a stricken voice: 'Jesus, Johnny, are you mad? You'll have us all in prison before the night is out. That was a police block, man!'

'A police block without police cars, police motorcycles or police uniforms: I wonder why the good Lord gave you pair two eyes apiece?'

Tweedledee said: 'But those police signs – '

'I will refrain from giving you pitying looks,' Harlow said kindly. 'Please do not overtax your minds. I would also point out that the French police do not wear masks, which this lot did, nor do they fix silencers to their guns.'

'Silencers?' The twins spoke as one.

'You heard those thumps and bumps on the back of the transporter? What do you think they were doing – throwing stones after us?'

Tweedledum said: 'Then what – '

'Hi-jackers. Members of an honoured and respected profession in these parts.' Harlow trusted he would be forgiven for this wicked slur on the honest citizens of Provence. But it was the best he could think of on the spur of the moment and, besides, the twins, though excellent mechanics, were of a rather simple cast of mind who would readily believe anything that a person of the stature of Johnny Harlow were to tell them.

'But how could they have known we were coming?'

'They didn't.' Harlow was improvising rapidly. 'They're usually in radio contact with lookouts posted a kilometre or so on either side of them. We've probably just passed the second one. When a likely-looking prospect – such as us – comes along it takes only a few seconds to have the lights in position and working.'

'A backward lot, those Froggies,' Tweedledum observed.

'Aren't they just? They haven't even got round to great train robberies yet.'

The twins composed themselves for slumber. Harlow, apparently tireless, was as alert and watchful as ever. After a few minutes, in his outside rear mirror, he caught sight of a pair of powerful headlights approaching at high speed. As they closed, Harlow briefly considered moving out to the middle of the road to block its passage just in case the occupant or occupants belonged to whatever opposition there might be but he dismissed the idea immediately. If they were ill-disposed, all they would have to do would be to shoot holes in his rear tyres at their leisure, as effective a way as any of bringing the transporter to a halt.

As it happened, the person or persons showed no signs of hostility, but one curious event occurred. As it overtook the transporter all the car's lights, both front and rear, went out and remained out until it was at least a hundred yards ahead, the driver of the car seeing by courtesy of the transporter's headlights: when its lights did come on again it was too far away for its rear numberplate to be identified.

Only seconds later, Harlow saw another pair of powerful headlights closing at even higher speed.

This car did not cut its lights as it overtook the transporter and it would have been most improbable had it done so for it was a police car with both siren and flashing blue light in splendid working order. Harlow permitted himself an almost beatific smile, and, just over a mile later, still had an expression of pleased anticipation on his face as he gently braked the transporter.

Ahead, the police car, blue lamp still flashing, was parked by the side of the road. Immediately ahead of it was another car, with a policeman, pad in hand, interrogating the driver through an opened window. There could be little question what the interrogation was about. Except on the autoroutes, the legal speed limit in France is 110 kph: the man being interrogated must have been doing at least 150 when he had passed the transporter. The transporter, still moving slowly, pulled out to the left to overtake both cars and Harlow had no difficulty in making out the number-plate of the front car. It read PNIIIK.

Like most major cities, Marseilles has places well worth looking at and others that do not qualify in that category. Certain sections of north-west Marseilles unmistakably belong in the latter category, seedy and rundown ex-suburban areas, now more industrial than they are residential. The rue Gerard was typical of such an area. While it might barely escape being described as an eye-sore, it was a singularly unprepossessing street almost entirely given over to small factories and large garages. The largest building in the street was a brick and corrugated iron monstrosity about half-way along on the left. Above the huge ribbed metal door was, in foot-high letters, the single word CORONADO.

As Harlow trundled the transporter down the rue Gerard he seemed unmoved by the unlovely spectacle before him. The twins were sound asleep. As Harlow approached the garage the metal door began to roll upwards and as Harlow swung out to make his approach, lights came on inside.

The garage was a cavernous place, eighty feet long and about fifty in width. It seemed ancient in construction and appearance but was about as well-kept, well-swept and clean as anyone could reasonably expect such a garage to be. Lined up against the right-hand wall were no fewer than three Coronado Formula I cars, and, pedestal-mounted beyond those, three unmistakable Ford-Cosworth V-8 engines. Nearest the door, on the same side, was a black Citroën DS21. The left-hand side of the garage was given over to rows of lavishly equipped work-benches while at the rear of the garage, stacked head-high, were dozens of crates of spares and tyres. Running both longitudinally and laterally were overhead beams for moving the engines about and for loading up the transporter.

Harlow eased the transporter in and stopped it precisely under the main longitudinal loading beam. He stopped the engine, shook the sleeping twins and climbed down to the garage floor. Jacobson was there to meet him. He didn't seem particularly glad to meet him but then Jacobson never seemed particularly glad to meet anyone. He looked at his watch and said grudgingly: 'Two o'clock. Fast trip.'

'Empty road. What now?'

'Bed. We've an old villa just round the corner. It's not much but it serves. We'll be here in the morning to start loading – after we unload, that is. The two resident mechanics will be here to help us.'

'Jacques and Harry?'

'They've left.' Jacobson looked even more sour than usual. 'Homesick, they said. They're always getting homesick. Homesick means too much hard work. New boys are Italian. Not half bad, though.'

Jacobson did not appear to have noticed the back of the transporter until then. He said: 'What the hell are those marks?'

'Bullets. Somebody tried to hi-jack us this side of Toulon. At least I think it was an attempted hi-jack but if it was they weren't very good at their job.'

'And why the hell should anyone want to hi-jack you? What good could a couple of Coronados be to anyone?'

'None. Maybe their information was wrong. This is the kind of wagon they use for transporting those very large cargoes of scotch or cigarettes. A million, two million francs a load – something really worth hi-jacking. Anyway, no harm done.

Fifteen minutes with a panel-beater and a spray gun and she'll be as good as new.'

'I'll report this to the police in the morning,' Jacobson said. 'Under French law it's an offence *not* to report such an incident. Not,' he added bitterly, 'that it will do any bloody good.'

The four men left the garage. As they did, Harlow glanced casually at the black Citroën. The number-plate read PNIIIK.

As Jacobson had said the old villa round the corner was not much but it served. Barely. Harlow sat in a chair by the side of a sparsely furnished room which, apart from a narrow bed and some worn linoleum, had as its only other item of furniture another chair which served as a bedside table. The window of the bedroom, which was on street level, had no curtains, just thin gauze netting. Although the room light was out, some faint degree of illumination was afforded by the weak street lights outside. Harlow twitched the netting fractionally aside and peered out. The mean, narrow little street outside, compared to which the rue Gerard was an arterial highway, was completely deserted.

Harlow glanced at his watch. The luminous hands said that it was two fifteen. Suddenly Harlow cocked his head, listening intently. It could have been his imagination, he thought; or perhaps what he heard was the sound of faint footfalls in the passageway outside. Noiselessly, he crossed to his bed and lay down on it. It did not creak because it was a flock mattress that had a long if probably dishonourable history behind it. His hand reached under the pillow, which was of the same vintage as the mattress, and brought out his black-jack. He slipped the thong over his right wrist then returned his right hand under the pillow.

The door opened stealthily. Breathing deeply and evenly, Harlow partly opened his eyes. A faint shadow stood in the doorway, but it was impossible to recognize who it was. Harlow remained as he was, perfectly relaxed and apparently soundly asleep. After a few seconds, the intruder closed the door as stealthily as he had opened it and Harlow's now highly attuned hearing could distinguish the soft sound of footsteps fading away. Harlow sat up, rubbing his chin in puzzled indecision, then left his bed and took up his vantage point by the window.

A man, this time clearly identifiable as Jacobson, had just left the house. He crossed the street and as he did so a dark car, a small Renault, rounded the corner and stopped almost directly opposite. Jacobson stooped and talked to the driver, who opened the door and stepped out. He removed his dark overcoat, folded it neatly – there was an unpleasant and rather menacing certainty about all his movements – placed it in the back seat, patted his pockets as if to reassure himself that nothing was missing, nodded to

Jacobson and began to cross the street. Jacobson walked away.

Harlow retreated to his bed, where he lay with his black-jacked right hand under his pillow, facing the window, his eyes fractionally open. Almost at once he saw a shadowy figure, his features indistinguishable because he was illuminated from behind, appear at the window and peer in. He brought up his right hand and examined what it held: there was nothing indistinguishable about this, it was a large and very unpleasant looking pistol, and as Harlow watched he slid back a catch on the side. It was then that Harlow saw that the gun had a lengthy cylindrical object screwed on to the end of the muzzle. A silencer, a piece of equipment designed to silence a shot for a fraction of a second and Harlow for ever. The figure disappeared.

Harlow left his bed with considerable alacrity. A blackjack, as compared to a silenced gun, had its distinct limitations. He crossed the room and took up position against the wall about two feet from the hinged side of the door.

For ten long seconds, which even Harlow found rather wearing on the nerves, there was total silence. Then there came the barely audible creak from a floor-board – the villa didn't go in much for deep-piled carpeting – in the passageway outside. The door handle depressed with almost millimetric stealth then slowly returned to position as the door, very very smoothly and gently, began to open. The gap between the door and jamb widened until it was about ten inches. Momentarily, the door ceased to move. A head began to poke its way cautiously through the gap. The intruder had a thin swarthy face, black hair plastered close to his narrow head and a pencil-line moustache.

Harlow leaned back on his left leg, raised his right leg and smashed the heel of his right foot against the door, just below the key-hole, from which the key had been thoughtfully and earlier removed. There was a muffled half-cough, half-scream of agony. Harlow jerked the door wide open and a short, thin dark-suited man stumbled into the room. Both hands, the right still clutching the gun, were clasped to the blood-masked shattered middle of his face. The nose was certainly broken: what had happened to cheekbones and teeth were, at the moment, a matter for the most idle conjecture.

It certainly didn't concern Harlow. His face was entirely without pity. He swung his black-jack, none too lightly, and brought it down over the intruder's right ear. Moaning, the man sank to his knees. Harlow took the gun from an unresisting hand and ran his free hand over the man's body. At his belt he discovered a sheath knife, which he withdrew. It was six inches long, double-edged, needle-pointed and razor-sharp. Gingerly, Harlow slipped the knife into his outside leather jacket pocket, changed his mind, switched over gun and knife, entwined his hand in the man's black greasy hair and pulled him ruthlessly to his feet. Equally ruthlessly, he pressed the blade of the knife into his back until he was sure the tip had penetrated the skin,

Harlow said: 'Outside.'

With the knife pressing ever deeper into his spine, Harlow's would-be killer had little option. The two men emerged from the villa and crossed the deserted street towards the little black Renault. Harlow pushed the man into the front seat while he himself got into the back.

Harlow said: 'Drive. Police.'

When the man spoke it was, understandably, with some muffled difficulty. He said: 'No can drive.'

Harlow reached for his black-jack and struck the man with approximately the same force as before but this time over the left ear. The man sagged wearily against the wheel.

Harlow said: 'Drive. Police.'

He drove, if his performance could be called driving. It was, understandably, the most erratic and harrowing journey Harlow had ever experienced. Apart from the fact that the man was barely conscious, he had to drive with one hand only, having to take his hand off the wheel to change gear, using the other hand to hold a blood-saturated handkerchief against his shattered face. Fortunately, the streets were deserted and the police station only ten minutes away.

Harlow half-pushed, half-carried the unhappy Italian into the station, deposited him not too gently on a bench, then went to the desk. Behind it were two large, burly and apparently genial policemen, both in uniform, one an inspector, the other a sergeant. They were studying with surprise and considerable interest the man on the bench who was now in a state of almost complete collapse, holding both hands to his blood-smeared face.

Harlow said: 'I want to lodge a complaint about this man.'

The inspector said mildly: 'It looks more to me that he should be lodging a complaint against you.'

Harlow said: 'You will be requiring some identification.' He pulled out his passport and driving licence but the inspector waved them away without even looking at them.

'Even to the police your face is better known than that of any criminal in Europe. But I had thought, Mr Harlow, that your sport was motor racing, not boxing.'

The sergeant, who had been studying the Italian with some interest, touched the inspector on the arm.

'Well, well, well,' he said, 'If it isn't our old friend and true, Luigi the Light-fingered. Difficult to recognize him, though.' He looked at Harlow. 'How did you make his acquaintance, sir?'

'He came visiting me. I'm sorry there was some violence.'

'Apologies are out of order,' the inspector said. 'Luigi should be beaten up regularly, preferably once a week. But this one should last him a couple of months. Was it – ah – necessary – ?'

Wordlessly, Harlow produced the knife and gun from his pockets and laid them on the counter.

The inspector nodded. 'With his record, a minimum of five years. You will press charges of course?'

'Please do if for me. I have urgent business. I'll look in later, if I may. Incidentally, I don't think Luigi came to rob me. I think he came to kill me. I'd like to find out who sent him.'

'I think that could be arranged, Mr Harlow.' There was a grim-faced thoughtfulness about the inspector that boded ill for Luigi.

Harlow thanked them, left, climbed into the Renault and drove off. Apart from the fact that he had no compunction in the world about borrowing Luigi's car, it was highly unlikely that its owner would be in any fit state to use it for quite some time to come. It had taken Luigi ten minutes to drive from the villa to the police station. It took Harlow just under four, and then less than another thirty seconds to be parked fifty yards away from the big roller door of the Coronado garage. The door was closed but bars of light could be seen on either side of it.

Fifteen minutes later Harlow stiffened and leaned forward. A small side door let into the main door had opened and four men emerged. Even in the negligible street lighting provided for the rue Gerard, Harlow had no difficulty in recognizing Jacobson, Neubauer and Tracchia. The fourth man he had never seen before: presumably he was one of Jacobson's mechanics. Jacobson left the closing and locking of the door to the others and walked quickly up the street in the direction of the villa. As he came abreast on the other side of the street, he didn't as much as glance in Harlow's direction. There are thousands of small black Renaults on the streets of Marseilles.

The other three men locked the door, climbed into a Citroën and drove off. Harlow's car, lightless, pulled away from the kerb and followed. It was to be in no sense a chase or pursuit, just two cars moving at a leisurely pace through the suburbs of the city, the one following the other at varying but always discreet distances. Only on one occasion did Harlow fall well back and switch on his side-lights at the sight of an approaching police car, but he had no difficulty in making up the lost ground.

Eventually, they came to a fairly broad tree-lined boulevard in an obviously well-to-do area. Large villas, hiding behind exceptionally high brick walls, lined both sides of the road. The Citroën rounded a right-angled corner. Fifteen seconds later Harlow did the same and immediately switched on his side-lights. About 150 yards ahead the Citroën had pulled up outside a villa and a man – it was Tracchia – had already left the car and was advancing towards the gates with a key in his hand. Harlow pulled out to overtake the parked car and as he did so he saw the gates swing open. The other two occupants of the Citroën ignored the passing Renault.

Harlow turned into the first side street and parked. He got out, pulled on Luigi's dark coat and lifted the collar high. He walked back to the boulevard which bore the corner name plate of rue Georges Sand and made his way along it till he came to the villa where the Citroën had turned in. It was called The Hermitage, a name that Harlow considered singularly inappropriate in the circumstances. The walls on either side of the gate were at least ten feet high, topped with broken bottle glass embedded in concrete. The gates were of the same height and had what appeared to be very sharp spikes on top. Twenty yards beyond the gates was the villa itself, a rambling old-fashioned Edwardian building much behung with balconies. Lights showed through chinks in the curtains on both floors.

Cautiously, Harlow tested the gates. They were locked. He glanced both ways to ensure that the boulevard was deserted, then produced a ring of fairly large keys. He studied the lock, studied the keys, selected one and tried it. It worked first time. He pocketed the keys and walked away.

Fifteen minutes later, Harlow parked his car in an undistinguished little street, almost an alleyway. He mounted a flight of street steps and at the top did not even have to knock or ring a bell. The door opened and an elderly man, plump, grey-haired and wrapped in a Chinese dressing-gown, beckoned him inside. The room into which he led Harlow seemed to be a cross between an electronic laboratory and a photographer's dark room. It was filled with, festooned with, impressively scientific-looking equipment which appeared to be of the most advanced kind. It did, however, possess two comfortable arm-chairs. The elderly man waved Harlow towards one of them.

He said: 'Alexis Dunnet warned me, but you *do* come at a most inconvenient hour, John Harlow. Pray, a seat.'

'I have come upon most inconvenient business, Giancarlo, and I haven't time to sit down.' He produced the film cassette and handed it over. 'How long to develop this and give me separate enlargements of each?'

'How many?'

'Frames, you mean?' Giancarlo nodded. 'Sixty. Give or take.'

'You do not ask for much.' Giancarlo was heavily sarcastic. 'This afternoon.'

Harlow said: 'Jean-Claude is in town?'

'Tsk! Tsk! Tsk! Code?' Harlow nodded. 'He is. I will see what he can do.'

Harlow left. On the way back to the villa he pondered the problem of Jacobson. Almost certainly the first thing that Jacobson would have done on his return to the villa would have been to check his, Harlow's, room. The absence of Harlow would have caused him no surprise at all: no worthwhile assassin was going to incriminate his employer by leaving a corpse in the room next to his: there were acres of water in and around Marseilles and heavy lead weights would not be difficult to come by if one knew where to look and Luigi the Light-fingered had given the distinct impression of one who wouldn't have had to look too far.

Jacobson was going to have a mild heart attack whether he met Harlow now or at the arranged meeting time of 6 a.m. But if he did not meet Harlow until 6 he was going to assume that Harlow had been absent until that time, and Jacobson, who was nothing if not suspicious, was going to wonder like fury what Harlow had been up to in the long watches of the night. It would be better to confront Jacobson now.

In the event, he had no option. He entered the villa just as Jacobson was about to leave it. Harlow regarded two things with interest: the bunch of keys dangling from Jacobson's hand – no doubt he was en route for the garage to perform some double-crossing operation on his friends and colleagues – and the look of utter consternation on the face of Jacobson, who must have been briefly and understandably under the impression that Harlow's ghost had come back to haunt him. But Jacobson was tough and his recovery, if not immediate, was made in a commendably short time.

'Four o'clock in the bloody morning!' Jacobson's shock showed through in his strained and over-loud voice. 'Where the hell have you been, Harlow?'

'You're not my keeper, Jacobson.'

'I bloody well am, too. I'm the boss now, Harlow. I've been looking and waiting for you for an hour. I was just about to contact the police.'

'Well, now, that *would* have been ironic. I've just come from them.'

'You've – what do you mean, Harlow?'

'What I say. I'm just back from handing over a thug to the police, a lad who came calling on me in the still watches of the night, gun and knife in hand. I don't think he came to tell me bed-time stories. He wasn't very good at his job. He'll be in bed now, a hospital bed, under heavy police guard.'

Jacobson said: 'Come inside. I want to hear more about this.'

They went inside and Harlow told Jacobson as much as he thought it was prudent for Jacobson to know of his night's activities, then said: 'God, I'm tired. I'll be asleep in one minute flat.'

Harlow returned to his spartan accommodation and took up watch by the window. In less than three minutes Jacobson appeared in the street, the bunch of keys still in his hand and headed in the direction of the rue Gerard, headed, presumably, for the Coronado garage. What his intentions were Harlow for the moment neither knew nor cared.

Harlow left the house and drove off in Luigi's Renault in a direction opposite to that which Jacobson had taken. After about four blocks, he turned into a narrow lane, stopped the engine, ensured that the doors were locked from the inside, set his wrist alarm for 5.45 a.m., and composed himself for a very brief sleep. As a place to lay his weary head Johnny Harlow had developed a powerful and permanent aversion to the Coronado villa.

CHAPTER NINE

It was just coming up for dawn when Harlow and the twins entered the Coronado garage. Jacobson and an unknown mechanic were already there. They looked, Harlow reflected, just as exhausted as he himself felt.

Harlow said: 'Thought you told me you had two new boys?'

'One of them didn't turn up. When he does,' Jacobson said grimly, 'he's out. Come on, let's empty the transporter and load up.'

The brilliant early morning sun, which presaged rain later in the day, was over the roof-tops when Harlow backed the transporter out into the rue Gerard. Jacobson said: 'On your way then, the three of you. I'll be in Vignolles about a couple of hours after you. Some business to attend to first.'

Harlow didn't even bother to make the natural inquiry as to what that business might be. In the first place he knew that whatever answer he got would be a lie. In the second place he knew what the answer was anyway: Jacobson would have an urgent appointment with his associates in The Hermitage in the rue Georges Sand to acquaint them with the misfortunes of Luigi the Light-fingered. So he merely contented himself with a nod and drove off.

To the twins' vast relief, the journey to Vignolles was not a replica of the hair-raising trip between Monza and Marseilles. Harlow drove almost sedately. In the first place, he had time in hand. Then again he knew he was so tired that he had lost the fine edge of his concentration. Finally, within an hour of leaving Marseilles, it had begun to rain, lightly at first then with increasing intensity, which drastically reduced visibility. Nevertheless, the transporter reached its destination by 11.30.

Harlow pulled the transporter to a stop mid-way between the stands and a large chalet-like building and climbed down, followed by the twins. It was still raining, and the skies were heavily overcast. Harlow gazed round the grey and empty desolation of the Vignolles track, stretched his arms and yawned.

'Home, sweet home. God, I'm tired. And hungry. Let's see what the canteen has to offer.'

The canteen had not, in fact, a great deal to offer but all three men were too hungry to complain. As they ate, the canteen slowly began to fill up, mainly with officials and employees of the track. Everyone knew Harlow, but almost no one acknowledged his presence. Harlow remained quite indifferent. At noon he pushed back his chair and made for the door and as he reached for the handle the door opened and Mary entered. She more than over-compensated for the general lack of welcome shown by the others. She smiled at him in delight, wrapped her arms around his neck and hugged him tightly. Harlow cleared his throat and looked round the canteen where the diners were now showing a vast degree more interest in him.

He said: 'I thought you said you were a very private person.'

'I am. But I hug everyone. You know that.'

'Well, thank you very much.'

She rubbed her cheek. 'You're scruffy, filthy and unshaven.'

'What do you expect of a face that hasn't seen water or felt a blade for twenty-four hours?'

She smiled. 'Mr Dunnet would like to see you in the chalet, Johnny. Though why he couldn't come to see you in the canteen – '

'I'm sure Mr Dunnet has his reasons. Such as not wanting to be seen in my company.'

She wrinkled her nose to show her disbelief and led the way out to the rain. She clung to his arm and said: 'I was so scared, Johnny. So scared.'

'And so you'd every right to be,' Harlow said solemnly. 'It's a perilous mission lugging a transporter to Marseilles and back.'

'Johnny.'

'Sorry.'

They hurried through the rain to the chalet, up the wooden steps, across the porch and into the hall. As the door closed, Mary reached for Harlow and kissed him. As a kiss, it was neither sisterly nor platonic. Harlow blinked his unresisting astonishment.

She said: 'But I don't do *that* to everyone. Or anyone.'

'You, Mary, are a little minx.'

'Ah, yes. But a lovable little minx.'

'I suppose so. I suppose so.'

Rory watched this scene from the head of the chalet stairs. He was scowling most dreadfully but had the wit to disappear swiftly as Mary and Harlow turned to mount the stairs: Rory's last meeting with Harlow was still a very painful memory.

Twenty minutes later, showered, shaved, but still looking very tired, Harlow was in Dunnet's room. The account of the night's activities he'd given to Dunnet had been brief, succinct, but had missed out nothing of importance.

Dunnet said: 'And now?'

'Straight back into Marseilles in the Ferrari. I'll check on Giancarlo and the films, then go and extend my sympathies to Luigi the Light-fingered'

'Will he sing?'

'Like a linnet. If he talks, the police will forget that they ever saw his gun and knife which will save our friend from five years' mail-bag sewing or breaking boulders in a quarry or whatever. Luigi does not strike me as the noblest Roman of them all.'

'How do you get back here?'

'By Ferrari.'

'But I thought that James said that – '

'That I was to leave it in Marseilles? I'm going to leave it in that disused farmyard down the road. I want the Ferrari tonight. I want to get into the Villa Hermitage tonight. I want a gun.'

For almost fifteen interminable seconds Dunnet sat quite still, not looking at Harlow, then he brought up his typewriter from beneath the bed, upended it and unclipped the base plate. This was lined with felt and was equipped with six pairs of spring clips. In the clips were held two automatic pistols, two silencers and two spare ammunition magazines. Harlow removed the smaller pistol, a silencer and a spare magazine. He pressed the magazine release switch, examined the magazine already in the gun and pressed it home again. He put all three items in the inner pocket of his leather jacket and zipped it up. He left the room without another word.

Seconds later he was with MacAlpine. MacAlpine's complexion was quite grey and he was unquestionably a very sick man with an illness insusceptible to physical diagnosis. He said: 'Leaving now? You must be exhausted.'

Harlow said: 'It'll probably hit me tomorrow morning.'

MacAlpine glanced through the window. The rain was sheeting down. He turned back to Harlow and said: 'Don't envy you your trip to Marseilles. But the forecast says it'll clear this evening. We'll unload the transporter then.'

'I think you're trying to say something, sir.'

'Well, yes.' MacAlpine hesitated. 'I believe you have been kissing my daughter.'

'That's a bare-faced lie. She was kissing me. Incidentally, one of these days I'm going to clobber that boy of yours.'

'You have my best wishes,' MacAlpine said wearily. 'Do you have designs upon my daughter, Johnny?'

'I don't know about that. But she sure as hell has designs on me.'

Harlow left and literally bumped into Rory in the corridor outside. They eyed each other, speculation in Harlow's eyes, trepidation in Rory's.

Harlow said: 'Aha! Eavesdropping again. Almost as good as spying, isn't it, Rory?'

'What? Me? Eavesdrop? Never!'

Harlow put a kindly arm around his shoulder.

'Rory, my lad, I have news. I not only have your father's permission for but approval of my intention to clobber you one of these days. At my convenience, of course.'

Harlow gave Rory a friendly pat on the shoulder: there was considerable menace in the friendliness. Harlow, smiling, descended the stairs to find Mary waiting.

She said: 'Speak to you, Johnny?'

'Sure. But on the porch. That black-haired young monster has probably got the whole place wired for sound.'

They went out on the porch, closing the door behind them. The chill rain was falling so heavily that it was impossible to see more than half-way across the abandoned airfield.

Mary said: 'Put your arm around me, Johnny.'

'I obediently put my arm round you. In fact, as a bonus, I'll put them both around you.'

'Please don't talk like that, Johnny. I'm scared. I'm scared all the time now, scared for you. There's something terribly wrong, isn't there, Johnny?'

'What should be wrong?'

'Oh, you are exasperating!' She changed the subject – or appeared to. 'Going to Marseilles?'

'Yes.'

'Take me with you.'

'No.'

'That's not very gallant.'

'No.'

'What *are* you, Johnny? What are you doing?'

She had been pressing closely against him but now she drew back, slowly, wonderingly. She put her hand inside his leather jacket, pulled the pocket zip and took out the automatic: she gazed down, hypnotized, at the blue metallic sheen of the gun.

'Nothing that's wrong, sweet Mary.'

She put her hand in his pocket again, took out the silencer and stared at it with eyes sick with worry and fear. She whispered: 'This is a silencer, isn't it? This way you can kill people without making a noise.'

'I said "Nothing that's wrong, sweet Mary."'

'I know. I know you never would. But – I must tell Daddy.'

'If you wish to destroy your father, then do so.' It was brutal, Harlow realized, but he knew of no other way. 'Go ahead. Tell him.'

'Destroy my – what do you mean?'

'There's something I want to do. If your father knew, he'd stop me. He's lost his nerve. Everybody's opinion to the contrary, I haven't lost mine.'

'What do you mean – destroy him?'

'I don't think he'd long survive the death of your mother.'

'My mother?' She stared at him for long seconds. 'But my mother – '

'Your mother's alive. I know she is. I think I can find out where she is. If I do, I'll go and get her tonight.'

'You're sure?' The girl was weeping silently. 'You're sure?'

'I'm sure, my sweet Mary.' Harlow wished he felt as confident as he sounded.

'There are police, Johnny.'

'No. I could tell them where to get the information but they wouldn't get it. They have to operate within the law.'

Instinctively, she dropped her brown tear-filled eyes from his and gazed at the gun and silencer in her hand. After a few moments she lifted her eyes again. Harlow nodded slightly, just once, took them gently from her, returned them to his pocket and closed the zip. She looked at him for a long moment, then took his leather lapels in her hands.

'Come back to me, Johnny.'

'I'll always come back to you, Mary.'

She tried to smile through her tears. It was not a very successful effort. She said: 'Another slip of the tongue?'

'That was not a slip of the tongue.' Harlow turned his leather collar high, descended the steps and walked quickly through the driving rain. He did not look back.

Less than one hour later Harlow and Giancarlo were occupying the two arm-chairs in Giancarlo's scientific laboratory. Harlow was leafing through a thick pile of glossy photographs. Harlow said: 'I'm a very competent cameraman, although I do say so myself.'

Giancarlo nodded. 'Indeed. And very full of human interest, those subjects of yours. We are, alas, temporarily baffled by the Tracchia and Neubauer documents, but then that makes them even more interesting, don't you think? Not that MacAlpine and Jacobson are lacking in interest. Far from it. Do you know that MacAlpine has paid out just over £140,000 in the past six months?'

'I guessed it was a lot – but *that* much! Even for a millionaire that must bite. What are the chances of identifying the lucky recipient?'

'At present, zero. It's a Zurich numbered account. But if they are presented with proved criminal acts, especially murder, the Swiss banks will open up.'

Harlow said: 'They'll get their evidence.'

Giancarlo looked at Harlow in lengthy speculation, then nodded. 'I should not be surprised. Now, as for our friend Jacobson, he must be the wealthiest mechanic in Europe. His addresses, incidentally, are those of the leading book-makers of Europe.'

'Gambling on the gee-gees?'

Giancarlo gave him a pitying look. 'No great feat to find what it was, the dates made it easy. Each lodgement was made two or three days after a Grand Prix race.'

'Well, well. An enterprising lad is our Jacobson. Opens up a whole new vista of fascinating possibilities, doesn't it?'

'Doesn't it, now? You can take those photographs. I have duplicates.'

'Thank you very much indeed.' Harlow handed back the photographs. 'Think I want to be caught with that bloody lot on me?'

Harlow said his thanks and goodbye and drove straight to the police station. On duty was the inspector who had been there in the early hours of the morning. His former geniality had quite deserted him: he now had about him a definitely lugubrious air.

Harlow said: 'Has Luigi the Light-fingered been singing sweet songs?'

The inspector shook his head sadly. 'Alas, our little canary has lost his voice.'

'Meaning?'

'His medicine did not agree with him. I fear, Mr Harlow, that you dealt with him in so heroic a fashion that he required pain-killing tablets every hour. I had four men guarding him – two outside the room, two inside. Ten minutes before noon this ravishingly beautiful young blonde nurse – that's how those cretins describe her – '

'Cretins?'

'My sergeant and his three men. She left two tablets and a glass of water and asked the sergeant to see that he took his medicine exactly at noon. Sergeant Fleury is nothing if not gallant so precisely at noon he gave Luigi his medicine.'

'What was the medicine?'

'Cyanide.'

It was late afternoon when Harlow drove the red Ferrari into the courtyard of the deserted farm just south of the Vignolles airfield. The door of the empty barn was open. Harlow took the car inside, stopped the engine and got out, trying to adjust his eyes to the gloom of the windowless barn. He was still trying to do this when a stocking-masked figure seemed to materialize out of this self-same gloom. Despite the almost legendary speed of his reactions Harlow had no time to get at his gun, for the figure was less than six feet away and already swinging what looked like a pick-axe handle. Harlow catapulted himself forward, getting in below the vicious swing of the club, his shoulder crashing into his assailant just below the breast-bone. The man, completely winded, gasped in agony, staggered backwards and fell heavily with Harlow on top of him, one hand on the prostrate man's throat while with the other he reached for his gun.

He did not even manage to get the gun clear of his pocket. He heard the faintest of sounds behind him and twisted round just in time to see another masked figure and a swinging club and catch the full impact of a vicious blow on the right forehead and temple. He collapsed without a sound. The man whom Harlow had winded climbed unsteadily to his feet and although still bent almost double in pain swung his leg and kicked Harlow full in his unconscious and unprotected face. It was perhaps fortunate for Harlow that his attacker was still in so weakened a state otherwise the kick might well have been lethal. Clearly, his attacker was dissatisfied with his initial effort for he drew his foot back again but his companion dragged him away before he could put his potentially lethal intentions into effect. The winded man, still bent over, staggered to and sat on a convenient bench while the other man proceeded to search the unconscious Harlow in a very thorough fashion indeed.

It was noticeably darker inside the barn when Harlow slowly began to come to. He stirred, moaned, then shakily raised shoulders and body off the ground until he was at arm's length from it. He remained in this position for some time then, with what was clearly a Herculean effort, managed to stagger to his feet where he remained uncontrollably swaying like a drunken man. His face felt as if it had been struck by a passing Coronado. After a minute or two, more by instinct than anything else, he lurched out of the garage, crossed the courtyard, falling down twice in the process, and made his erratic way towards the airfield tarmac.

The rain had now stopped falling and the sky was beginning to clear. Dunnet had just emerged from the canteen and was heading towards the chalet when he caught sight of this staggering figure, less than fifty yards away, weaving its seemingly alcoholic way across the airfield tarmac. For a moment Dunnet stood like a man turned to stone, then broke into a dead run. He reached Harlow in seconds, put a supporting arm around his shoulders as he stared into his face, a face now barely recognizable. The forehead was wickedly gashed and hideously bruised and the blood that had seeped – and was still seeping – had completely masked the right side of his face and blinded his right eye. The left-hand side of the face was in little better condition. The left cheek was one huge bruise with a transverse cut. He bled from nose and mouth, his lip was split and at least two teeth were missing.

'Christ Almighty!' Dunnet said. 'Dear Christ Almighty!'

Dunnet half-guided, half-carried the staggering, semiconscious Harlow across the tarmac, up the steps, across the porch and into the hall of the chalet. Dunnet cursed under his breath as Mary chose just that moment to emerge from the living-room. She stood stock-still for a moment, brown eyes huge in a white appalled face, and when she spoke her voice was a barely audible whisper.

'Johnny!' she said. 'Oh, Johnny, Johnny, Johnny. What have they done to you?'

She reached forward and gently touched the blood-masked face, beginning to tremble uncontrollably as the tears rolled down her face.

'No time for tears, Mary, my dear.' Dunnet's voice was deliberately brisk. 'Warm water, sponge, towel. After that, bring the first-aid box. On no account are you to tell your father. We'll be in the lounge.'

Five minutes later, in the lounge, a basin of bloodstained water and a bloodstained towel lay at Harlow's feet. His face was clear of blood now and the end result was, if anything, worse looking than ever inasmuch as the gashes and bruises stood out in clear relief. Dunnet, ruthlessly applying iodine and antiseptics, was taping up the gashes and from the frequent wincing expressions on the face of his patient, it was clear that Harlow was suffering considerably. He put finger and thumb inside his mouth, wrenched, winced again and came out with a tooth which he regarded with disfavour before dropping into the basin. When he spoke, despite the thickness of his speech, it was clear that however damaged he might have been physically, mentally he was back on balance.

'You and me, Alexis. I think we should have our photographs taken. For the family albums. How do we compare for looks?'

Dunnet examined him judicially. 'About even-stephen, I should say.'

'True, true. Mind you, I think nature gave me an unfair start over you.'

'Stop it, stop it, will you.' Mary was openly crying. 'He's hurt, he's terribly hurt. I'm going to get a doctor.'

'No question.' The bantering note had left Harlow's voice and there was iron in it now. 'No doctors. No stitches. Later. Not tonight.'

Mary, her eyes brimming with tears, gazed fixedly at the glass of brandy Harlow held in his hand. The hand was steady as that of a stone statue. She said, not with bitterness, only a dawning of understanding: 'You fooled us all. The nerve-shattered world champion with the shaking hands. You fooled us all the time. Didn't you, Johnny?'

'Yes. Please leave the room, Mary.'

'I swear I'll never talk. Not even to Daddy.'

'Leave the room.'

'Leave her be,' Dunnet said. 'If you talk, Mary, you know he'd never look at you again. My God, it never rains but it pours. You're our second alarm this afternoon. Tweedledum and Tweedledee are missing.'

Dunnet looked at Harlow for his reaction but there was none.

Harlow said: 'They were working on the transporter at the time.' It was a statement, not a question.

'How the hell do you know?'

'In the south hangar. With Jacobson.'

Dunnet nodded slowly.

'They saw too much,' Harlow said. 'Too much. It must have been by accident because God knows they weren't overburdened by intelligence. But they saw too much. What's Jacobson's story?'

'The twins went for a tea-break. When they didn't come back after forty minutes, he went looking for them. They'd just vanished.'

'Did they, in fact, go to the canteen?' Dunnet shook his head. 'Then if they're ever found it will be in the bottom of a ravine or a canal. Remember Jacques and Henry in the Coronado garage?' Dunnet nodded. 'Jacobson said they'd become homesick and gone home. They've gone home all right – in the same way that Tweedledum and Tweedledee have gone home. He's got two new mechanics down there but only one turned up for work this morning. The other didn't. I've no proof, but I'll get it. The missing lad didn't turn up because I put him in hospital in the middle hours of the night.'

Dunnet showed no reaction. Mary stared at Harlow with unbelieving horror in her eyes.

Harlow went on: 'Sorry, Mary. Jacobson is a killer, murderer if you like. He'll stop at nothing to protect his own interests. I know he was responsible for the death of my young brother in the first Grand Prix of this season. That was what first made Alexis persuade me to work for him.'

Mary said in total disbelief: 'You work for Alexis? A journalist?'

Harlow went on as if he had not heard her. 'He tried to kill me in the French Grand Prix. I have photographic proof. He was responsible for Jethou's death. He tried to get me last night by using a fake police trap to stop the transporter. He was responsible for the murder of a man in Marseilles today.'

Dunnet said calmly: 'Who?'

'Luigi the Light-fingered. He was fed a pain-reliever in hospital today. It certainly removed him from all pain – permanently. Cyanide. Jacobson was the only person who knew about Luigi so he had him eliminated before he could sing to the police. My fault – I'd told Jacobson. My fault. But I'd no option at the time.'

'I can't believe it.' Mary was totally bewildered. 'I *can't* believe it. This is a nightmare.'

'Believe what you like. Just stay a mile away from Jacobson. He'll read your face like a book and will begin to become very interested in you. I should hate for Jacobson to become very interested in you, I'd rather you didn't end up in a gravel pit. And always remember – you're crippled for life and Jacobson did it.'

While he had been talking, Harlow had been carrying out a thorough examination of his pockets.

'Cleaned out,' he said matter-of-factly. 'Completely. Wallet, passport, driving licence, money, car keys – but I have spares. All my skeleton keys.' He pondered briefly. 'That means I'll require a rope, hook and tarpaulin from the transporter. And then – '

Mary interrupted, fear in her eyes. 'You're not – you can't go out again tonight! You should be in hospital.'

Harlow glanced at her briefly, expressionlessly, then went on: 'And then, of course, they took my gun. I shall require another, Alexis. And some money.'

Harlow pushed himself to his feet, walked quickly and quietly to the door and jerked it open. Rory, who had clearly been listening with his ear pressed hard against the door, more or less fell into the room. Harlow seized him by the hair and Rory yelped in agony as Harlow straightened him up.

Harlow said: 'Look at my face, Rory.'

Rory looked, winced and the colour drained from his own.

Harlow said: 'You're responsible for that, Rory.'

Suddenly, without warning, he struck Rory flat-handed across the left cheek. It was a heavy blow and would normally have sent Rory reeling but he couldn't in this case because Harlow's left hand was firmly entwined in his hair. Harlow struck him again, backhanded and with equal force, across the right cheek, then proceeded to repeat the process with metronomic regularity.

Mary screamed: 'Johnny! Johnny! Have you gone mad?' She made to throw herself at Harlow but Dunnet moved swiftly to pin her arms from behind. Dunnet appeared remarkably unperturbed by the turn events had taken.

'I'm going to keep this up, Rory,' Harlow said, 'until you feel the way I look.'

Harlow kept it up. Rory made no attempt to resist or retaliate. His head was beginning to roll from side to side, quite helplessly, as Harlow continued to strike him repeatedly. Then, considering that the softening-up process had probably gone far enough, Harlow stopped.

Harlow said: 'I want information. I want the truth. I want it now. You eavesdropped on Mr Dunnet and myself this afternoon, did you not?'

Rory's voice was a trembling pain-wracked whisper. 'No ! No! I swear I didn't. I swear – '

He broke off with a screech of pain as Harlow resumed the treatment. After a few seconds Harlow stopped again. A sobbing Mary, still securely held by Dunnet, was looking at him in stupefied horror.

Harlow said: 'I was beaten up by some people who knew I was going to Marseilles to see about some very important pictures. They wanted those pictures very very badly. They also knew that I would be parking the Ferrari in a barn in a disused farmhouse a little way down the road. Mr Dunnet was the only other person who knew about the pictures and the farmyard. You think perhaps he told?'

'Maybe.' Like his sister's, Rory's cheeks were now liberally streaked with tears. 'I don't know. Yes, yes, he must have done.'

Harlow spoke slowly and deliberately, interspersing every other few words with a resounding slap.

'Mr Dunnet is not a journalist. Mr Dunnet has never been an accountant. Mr Dunnet is a senior officer of the Special Branch of New Scotland Yard and a member of Interpol and he has accumulated enough evidence against you, for aiding and abetting criminals, to ensure that you'll spend the next few years in a remand home and Borstal.' He removed his left hand from Rory's hair. 'Whom did you tell, Rory?'

'Tracchia.'

Harlow pushed Rory into an arm-chair where he sat hunched, his hands covering his aching scarlet face.

Harlow looked at Dunnet. 'Where's Tracchia?'

'Gone to Marseilles. He said. With Neubauer.'

'He was out here, too ? He would be. And Jacobson?'

Out in his car. Looking for the twins. He said.'

'He's probably taken a spade with him. I'll get the spare keys and fetch the Ferrari. Meet you at the transporter in fifteen minutes. With the gun. And money.'

Harlow turned and walked away. Rory, rising rather unsteadily to his feet, followed. Dunnet put an arm round Mary's shoulders, pulled out a breast handkerchief and proceeded to clean her tear-ravaged face. Mary looked at him in wonderment.

'Are you what Johnny said you were? Special Branch? Interpol?'

'Well, yes, I'm a police officer of sorts.'

'Then stop him, Mr Dunnet. I beg of you. Stop him.'

'Don't you know your Johnny yet?'

Mary nodded miserably, waited until Dunnet had effected his running repairs, then said: 'He's after Tracchia, isn't he?'

'He's after Tracchia. He's after a lot of people. But the person he's really after is Jacobson. If Johnny says that Jacobson is directly responsible for the deaths of seven people, then he's directly responsible for the deaths of seven people. Apart from that he has two personal scores to settle with Jacobson.'

'His young brother?' Dunnet nodded. 'And the other?'

'Look at your left foot, Mary.'

CHAPTER TEN

At the roundabout south of Vignolles, a black Citroën braked to give precedence to Harlow's red Ferrari. As the Ferrari swept by, Jacobson, at the wheel of the Citroën, rubbed his chin thoughtfully, turned his car towards Vignolles and stopped by the first roadside telephone booth.

In the Vignolles canteen MacAlpine and Dunnet were finishing a meal in the now almost deserted room. They were both looking towards the door, watching Mary leave.

MacAlpine sighed. 'My daughter is in low spirits tonight.'

'Your daughter is in love.'

'I fear so. And where the hell has that young devil Rory got to?'

'Well, not to put too fine a point on it, Harlow caught that young devil eavesdropping.'

'Oh, no. Not again?'

'Again. The ensuing scene was quite painful really. I was there. I rather think that Rory was afraid that he might find Johnny here. Johnny, in fact, is in bed – I don't think he'd any sleep last night.'

'And that sounds a very attractive proposition to me. Bed, I mean. I feel unaccountably tired tonight. If you will excuse me, Alexis.'

He half rose to his feet, then sat down again as Jacobson entered and approached their table. He looked very tired indeed.

MacAlpine said: 'What luck?'

'Zero. I've searched everywhere within five miles of here. Nothing. But I've just had a report from the police that two people answering closely to their descriptions have been seen in Le Beausset – and there can't be many people around like the terrible twins. I'll just have a bite and go there. Have to find a car first, though. Mine's on the blink – hydraulics gone.'

MacAlpine handed Jacobson a set of car keys. 'Take my Aston.'

'Well, thank you, Mr MacAlpine. Insurance papers?'

'Everything in the glove box. Very kind of you to go to such trouble, I must say.'

They're my boys too, Mr MacAlpine.'

Dunnet gazed expressionlessly into the middle distance.

* * *

The Ferrari's speedometer registered 180 kph. Harlow was clearly paying scant attention to the French 110 kph restriction, but from time to time, purely from instinct, for it seemed unlikely that there was any police car in France capable of overtaking him, he consulted his rear mirror. But there was at no time anything to be seen except the coils of rope, hook and first-aid box on the back seat and the hump of a dirty white tarpaulin which had been clearly flung carelessly on the floor.

An incredible forty minutes after leaving Vignolles the Ferrari passed the Marseilles sign. A kilometre farther on the Ferrari pulled up as traffic lights changed to red. Harlow's face was so battered and bruised and covered in plaster that it was impossible to tell what expression it wore. But the eyes were as calm and steady and watchful as ever, his posture as immobile as ever: no impatience, no drumming of fingers on the wheel. But even Harlow's total relaxation could be momentarily upset.

'Mr Harlow.' The voice came from the rear of the car.

Harlow swung round and stared at Rory, whose head had just emerged from its cocoon of canvas tarpaulin. When Harlow spoke it was with slow, deliberate, spaced words.

'What the hell are you doing there?'

Rory said defensively: 'I thought you might be needing a bit of a hand, like.'

Harlow restrained himself with what was obviously an immense effort.

'I could say 'This is all I need' but I don't think that would help much.' From an inner pocket he fished out some of the money that Dunnet had given him. 'Three hundred francs. Get a hotel and phone Vignolles for a car in the morning.'

'No, thank you, Mr Harlow. I made a terrible mistake about you. I'm just plain stupid, I guess. I won't say sorry, for all the sorries in the world are not enough. The best way to say "sorry" is to help. Please, Mr Harlow.'

'Look, laddie, I'll be meeting people tonight, people who would kill you soon as look at you. And now I'm responsible for you to your father.'

The lights changed and the Ferrari moved on. What little could be seen of Harlow's face looked slightly bemused.

'And that's another thing,' Rory said. 'What's wrong with him? My father, I mean.'

'He's being blackmailed.'

'Dad? Blackmailed?' Rory was totally incredulous.

'Nothing he's ever done. I'll tell you some time.'

'Are you going to stop those people from blackmailing him?'

'I hope so.'

'And Jacobson. The man who crippled Mary. I must have been mad to think it was your fault. Are you going to get him, too?'

'Yes.'

'You didn't say "I hope so" this time. You said "Yes".'

'That's right.'

Rory cleared his throat and said diffidently: 'You going to marry Mary, Mr Harlow?'

'The prison walls appear to be closing round me.'

'Well, I love her too. Different like, but just as much. If you're going after the bastard who crippled Mary I'm coming too.'

'Watch your language,' Harlow said absently. He drove some way in silence then sighed in resignation. 'OK. But only if you promise to stay out of sight and keep safe.'

'I'll stay out of sight and keep safe.'

Harlow made to bite his upper lip and winced as he bit the gash in that lip. He looked in the rear mirror. Rory, now sitting on the back seat, was smiling with considerable satisfaction. Harlow shook his head in what might have been disbelief or despair or both.

Ten minutes later Harlow parked the car in an alleyway about three hundred yards away from the rue Georges Sand, packed all the equipment into a canvas bag, slung it over his shoulder and set off, accompanied by a Rory whose expression of complacency had now changed to one of considerable apprehension. Other factors apart, there was a sound enough reason for Rory's nervousness. It was a bad night for the purposes Harlow had in mind. A full moon hung high in a cloudless starlit Riviera sky. The visibility was at least as good as it would have been on an overcast winter's afternoon. The only difference was that moon-shadows are much darker.

Harlow and Rory were now pressed close into the shadow of one of the ten-foot high walls that surrounded the Villa Hermitage. Harlow examined the contents of the bag.

'Now then. Rope, hook, tarpaulin, twine, insulated wire-cutters, chisels, first-aid box. Yes, the lot.'

'What is that lot for, Mr Harlow?'

'First three for getting over that wall. Twine for tying things up or together, like thumbs. Wire-cutters for electric alarms – if I can find the wires. Chisels for opening things. First-aid box – well, you never know. Rory, will you kindly stop your teeth from chattering? Our friends inside could hear you forty feet away.'

'I can't help it, Mr Harlow.'

'Now, remember, you're to stay here. The last people we want here are the police but if I'm not back in thirty minutes go to the phone box on the corner and tell them to come here at the double.'

Harlow secured the hook to the end of the rope. For once, the bright moonlight was of help. With his first upward cast the hook sailed over the branch of a tree within the grounds. He pulled cautiously until the hook engaged firmly round the branch, slung the white tarpaulin over his shoulder, climbed the few feet that were necessary, draped the tarpaulin over the broken glass embedded in the concrete, pulled himself farther up, sat gingerly astride and looked at the tree that had provided this convenient branch: the lower branches extended to within four feet of the ground.

Harlow glanced down at Rory. 'The bag.'

The bag came sailing upwards. Harlow caught it and dropped it on the ground inside. He took the branch in his hands, swung inwards and was on the ground in five seconds.

He passed through a small thicket of trees. Lights shone from the curtained windows of a ground floor room. The massive oaken door was shut and almost certainly bolted. In any event Harlow considered that a frontal entry was as neat a way as any of committing suicide. He approached the side of the house, keeping to shadows wherever possible. The windows on the ground floor offered no help – all were heavily barred. The back door, predictably, was locked: the ironic thought occurred to Harlow that the only skeleton keys which could have probably opened that door were inside that house.

He moved round to the other side of the house. He didn't even bother looking at the barred lower windows. He looked upwards and his attention was at once caught and held by a window that was slightly ajar. Not much, perhaps three inches, but still ajar. Harlow looked around the grounds. About twenty yards away were a cluster of garden and potting sheds and a greenhouse. He headed resolutely in their direction.

Rory, meanwhile, was pacing up and down in the lane outside, continually glancing at the rope in what appeared to be an agony of indecision. Suddenly, he seized the rope and began to climb.

By the time he had dropped to the ground on the other side, Harlow had a ladder against the lower sill of the window and had reached the level of the window itself. He pulled out his torch and carefully examined both sides of the window. Both sides had what were clearly electrical wires stapled to the framework of the window. Harlow reached inside his bag, produced the wire-cutters, snipped both wires, lifted the sash high and passed inside.

Within two minutes he had established that there was no one on the upper floor. Canvas bag and unlit torch in his left hand, the silenced pistol in the other, he stealthily descended the stairs towards the hallway. Light streamed from a door that was slightly ajar and the sound of voices from inside, one of them a woman's, carried very clearly. This room he temporarily ignored. He prowled round the ground floor ensuring that all the rooms were empty. In the kitchen, his torch located a set of steps leading down to the basement. Harlow descended those and played his torch round a concrete-floored, concrete-walled cellar. Four doors led off this cellar. Three of those looked perfectly normal: the fourth had two massive bolts and a heavy key such as one might expect to find in a medieval dungeon. Harlow slid the bolts, turned the key, passed inside, located and pressed a light switch.

Whatever it was, it was certainly no dungeon. It was a very modern and immaculately equipped laboratory although what precisely it was equipped to do was not immediately apparent. Harlow crossed to a row of aluminium containers, lifted the lid of one, sniffed the white powdery contents, wrinkled his nose in disgust and replaced the lid. As he left he passed by a wall telephone, obviously, from the dial, an external exchange one. He hesitated, shrugged and walked out, leaving the door open and the light on.

Rory, just at the precise moment when Harlow was mounting the steps from the cellar, was hidden in the deep shadow on the edge of the thicket of trees. From where he stood he could see both the front and the side of the house. His face held a considerable degree of apprehension, an apprehension that suddenly changed to something very close to fear.

A squat, powerfully built man, clad in dark trousers and a dark roll-neck pullover, had suddenly appeared from behind the back of the house. For a moment the man, the patrolling guard that Harlow hadn't bargained for, stood stock-still, staring at the ladder propped against the wall. Then he started running towards the front door of the house. As if by magic two items had appeared in his hands – a large key and a very much larger knife.

Harlow stood in the hallway outside the occupied room, thoughtfully regarding the bar of light streaming from the partially opened door and listening to the sound of voices. He tightened the silencer on his gun, took two quick steps forward then violently smashed the door open with the sole of his right foot: the door all but parted company with its hinges.

There were five people inside the room. Three of them were curiously alike and might well have been brothers – heavy, well-suited, obviously prosperous men, black-haired and very swarthy. The fourth was a beautiful blonde girl. The fifth was Willi Neubauer. They stared as if mesmerized at Harlow who, with his bruised and battered face and silenced pistol, must have presented a less than friendly appearance.

Harlow said: 'The hands high, please.'

All five lifted their hands.

'Higher. Higher.'

The five occupants of the room stretched their arms very high indeed.

'What the devil does this mean, Harlow?' Neubauer's tone was intended to be harsh and demanding but it burred with the sharp edge of strain. 'I come calling on friends – '

Harlow interrupted in an iron voice. 'The judge will have more patience with you than I have. Shut up!'

'Look out!' The almost panic-stricken scream was barely recognizable as Rory's voice.

Harlow had the cat-like reflexes that befitted the outstanding Grand Prix driver of his time. He turned and fired in one movement. The dark man, who had been just about to start a vicious down-stroke, screamed in agony and stared in disbelief at his shattered hand. Harlow ignored him and had whirled back to face the others even before the dark man's knife had struck the floor. One of the swarthy men had dropped his right hand and was reaching inside his jacket.

Harlow said encouragingly: 'Go on.'

The swarthy man lifted his right hand very quickly indeed. Harlow stepped prudently to one side and gestured briefly with his gun towards the wounded man.

'Join your friends.' Moaning in pain, his left hand clutching his bleeding right, the dark man did so. Just then Rory entered the room.

Harlow said: 'Thank you, Rory. All sins forgiven. Get the first-aid box from that bag. I told you we might need it.' He surveyed the company coldly. 'And I do hope this is the last time we need it.' He pointed his gun at the blonde girl. 'Come here, you.'

She rose from her chair and came slowly forward. Harlow smiled at her, chillingly, but she was either too shocked or stupid to realize what lay behind that smile.

'I believe you have some pretensions towards being a nurse,' Harlow said, 'even though the late and un-lamented Luigi might not agree with that. There's the first-aid box. Fix your friend's hand.'

She spat at him. 'Fix it yourself.'

Harlow gave no warning. There was a blur of movement and the silencer of the pistol smashed against the blonde's face. She screamed, staggered and fell to a sitting position, blood welling from gashes on both cheek and mouth.

'Jesus!' Rory was appalled. 'Mr Harlow!'

'If it's any consolation, Rory, this charmer is wanted for premeditated murder.' He looked at the blonde and what little could be seen of his face was totally devoid of pity. 'Get to your feet and fix your friend's hand. Then, if you wish, your own face. Not that I care. The rest of you, face down on the floor, hands behind your back. Rory, see if they have guns. The first man that as much as twitches will be shot through the back of the head.'

Rory searched them. When he had finished, he looked down almost in awe at the four guns he had placed on the table.

'They *all* had guns, 'he said.

'What did you expect them to be carrying? Powder puffs? Now, Rory, the twine. You know what to do. As many knots as you like, the twine as tight as possible and the hell with their circulation.' Rory set about his task with enthusiasm and in very short order had the hands of all six securely bound behind their backs: the dark man now had his hand roughly bandaged.

Harlow said to Neubauer: 'Where's the gate key?'

Neubauer glared venomously and kept silent. Harlow pocketed his gun, picked up the knife his would-be assailant had dropped and pressed the tip against Neubauer's throat, just breaking the skin.

'I'm going to count three then I'm going to push this knife clear through to the back of your neck. One. Two.'

'Hall table.' Neubauer's face was ashen.

'On your feet, all of you. Down to the cellar.'

They trooped down to the cellar, all with highly apprehensive expressions on their faces. So apprehensive was the last of the six, one of the three swarthy men, that he made a sudden vicious lunge at Harlow, probably with the intention of knocking him down the steps and then stamping on him, which was a very foolish thing to do, for he had already had eye-witness proof of the quite remarkable speed of Harlow's reactions. Harlow stepped nimbly to one side, struck him above the ear with the barrel of his pistol and watched him topple then fall halfway down the steps. Harlow caught one of his ankles and dragged him down the lower half of the stairs, the unconscious man's head bumping from concrete step to concrete step.

One of the other swarthy men shouted: 'God's sake, Harlow, are you mad ? You'll kill him!'

Harlow dragged the unconscious man down the last step until his head hit the concrete floor and looked indifferently at the man who had made the protest. 'So? I'm probably going to have to kill you all anyway.'

He ushered them into the cellar laboratory and, with Rory's assistance, dragged the unconscious man in after them.

Harlow said: 'Lie down on the floor. Rory, tie their ankles together. Very tightly, please.' Rory did so, displaying not only enthusiasm for but now positive enjoyment in his work. When he had finished, Harlow said: 'Go through their pockets. See what identification papers they are carrying. Not Neubauer. We all know who our dear Willi is.'

Rory returned to Harlow with quite a bundle of identification documents in his hand. He looked uncertainly at the woman on the floor. 'What about the lady, Mr Harlow?'

'Never confuse that murderous bitch with a lady.' Harlow looked at her. 'Where's your handbag?'

'I haven't got a handbag.'

Harlow sighed, crossed to where she lay and knelt beside her. 'When I'm finished with the other side of your face no man will ever look at you again. Not that you'll be seeing any men for a long time to come – no court is going to overlook the testimony of four policemen who can identify you and the fingerprints on that glass.' He looked at her consideringly then lifted his gun. 'And I don't suppose the wardresses will care what you look like. Where's that handbag?'

'In my bedroom.' The tremble in her voice accurately reflected the fear in her face.

'Where in your bedroom?'

'The wardrobe.'

Harlow looked at Rory. 'Rory, if you would be so kind.'

Rory said uncertainly: 'How will I know which bedroom?'

Harlow said patiently: 'When you come to a bedroom where the dressing-table looks like the toilet counter in a pharmacy, then you'll have found the right bedroom. And bring down the four guns from the living-room.'

Rory left. Harlow got to his feet, crossed to the desk where he'd placed the identification documents and began to study those with interest. After about a minute he looked up.

'Well, well, well. Marzio, Marzio and Marzio. Sounds like a firm of well-established solicitors. And all from Corsica. I seem to have heard of the Marzio brothers before. I'm quite certain the police have and will be delighted to have those documents.' He laid down the papers, pulled six inches of a roll of stand-mounted Scotch tape and affixed it lightly to the edge of the desk. He said: 'You'll never guess what that's for.'

Rory returned, bearing with him a handbag so large as to be more a valise than a handbag, along with four guns. Harlow opened the bag, examined the contents, which included a passport, then unzipped only a side compartment and pulled out a gun.

'My, my. So Anne-Marie Puccelli carries a fire-arm around with her. No doubt to fend off those would-be nasty attackers bent on robbing her of those cyanide tablets such as she fed to the late Luigi.' Harlow replaced the gun, then dropped into the bag the other documents and the four guns Rory had brought. He extracted the first-aid box from the bag, took out a very small bottle and poured white tablets into his hand.

'How convenient. Exactly six tablets. One for each. I want to know where Mrs MacAlpine is being held and I'm going to know in less than two minutes. Florence Nightingale there will know what those are.'

Florence Nightingale had no comment to make. Her face was paper-white and drawn, she appeared to have put on ten years in ten minutes.

Rory said: 'What are those things?'

'Sugar-coated cyanide. Quite pleasant to take really. Take about three minutes to melt.'

'Oh, no ! You *can't* do that.' Shock had drained Rory's face of all its colour. 'You just can't. That – that's *murder.*'

'You want to see your mother again, don't you? Besides, it's not murder, it's extermination. We're dealing with animals, not human beings. Look around you. What do you think the end product of this charming old cottage industry is?' Rory shook his head. He seemed to be completely numbed. 'Heroin. Think of the hundreds, more likely thousands, of people they've killed. I insulted animals by calling them animals. They're the lowest form of vermin on earth. It would be a pleasure to wipe out all six of them.'

Among the six bound, prostrate prisoners there was a considerable amount of sweating and lip-licking in evidence. All six were plainly terrified. There was a ruthless implacibility in Harlow that made it all too horrifyingly plain that he was in deadly earnest.

Harlow knelt on Neubauer's chest, tablet in one hand, gun, in the other. He struck Neubauer, stiff-fingered, in the solar plexus. Neubauer gasped and Harlow stuck the silencer of his pistol into his opened mouth so preventing him from clenching his teeth. With finger and thumb he held the tablet alongside the silencer.

Harlow said: 'Where is Mrs MacAlpine?' He withdrew the gun. Neubauer was babbling, almost mad with fear.

'Bandol! Bandol! Bandol! In a boat.'

'What type? Where?'

'In the bay. Motor yacht. Forty feet or so. Blue with white top. *The Chevalier* it's called.'

Harlow said to Rory: 'Bring me that strip of Scotch tape from the side of the table.' He repeated his two-fingered assault on Neubauer's solar plexus. Once again the gun was in the mouth. Harlow dropped the tablet in. 'I don't believe you.' He strapped the tape across Neubauer's mouth. 'Just to prevent you from spitting that cyanide tablet out.'

Harlow moved across to the man who had made the vain attempt to pull his gun. Tablet in hand, he sank to his knees. Totally panic-stricken, the man started screaming at Harlow before the latter could speak.

'Are you mad? Are you mad? For God's sake, it's true! *The Chevalier.* Bandol. Blue and white. She's anchored two hundred metres off-shore.'

Harlow stared at the man for a long moment, nodded, rose, crossed to the wall phone, lifted the receiver and dialled 17 – *Police secours,* which can be variously interpreted as police-help or police-emergency. He made contact almost instantly.

Harlow said: 'I'm speaking from the Villa Hermitage in the rue Georges Sand. Yes, that's it. In a basement room you will find a fortune in heroin. In the same room you will find the equipment for the bulk manufacture of heroin. Also in the same room you will find six people responsible for the manufacture and distribution of this heroin. They will offer no resistance – they are securely bound. Three of them are the Marzio brothers. I have taken their identification papers along with those of a wanted murderess called Anne-Marie Puccelli. These will be given to you later tonight.' There came from the earpiece the sound of a voice talking rapidly, urgently, but Harlow ignored it. He said: 'I will not repeat myself. I know that every emergency call is tape-recorded, so there's no point in trying to detain me until you get here.' He hung up, to find Rory gripping his arm.

Rory said desperately: 'You've got your information. The three minutes aren't up. You could still get that tablet from Neubauer's mouth.'

'Ah, that.' Harlow put four of the tablets back in the small bottle, held up the fifth, 'five grains acetylsalicylic acid. Aspirin. That's why I taped his mouth – I didn't want him shouting to his pals that all he had been fed was an aspirin – there can't be an adult human being in the western world who doesn't know the taste of aspirin. Look at his face – he's not terrified any more, he's just hopping mad. Come to that, they all look hopping mad. Ah, well.' He picked up the girl's handbag and looked at her. 'We'll borrow this temporarily – fifteen, twenty years, whatever the judge cares to give you.'

They left, bolting and locking the door behind them, took the gate key from the hall table, ran through the open front door, down the driveway then unlocked and opened the gates. Harlow pulled Rory into the shadow of a cluster of pine trees.

Rory said: 'How long do we stay here?'

'Just till we make sure that the right people get here first.'

Only seconds later they heard the ululating wails of approaching sirens. Very shortly afterwards, sirens still on and lights flashing, two police cars and a police van came at speed through the gateway and pulled up in a shower of spraying gravel and at least seven policemen ran up the steps and through the open doorway. Despite

Harlow's reassurance that the prisoners had been immobilized, they all considered it necessary to have their guns in their hands.

Harlow said: 'The right people got here first.'

Fifteen minutes later, Harlow was seated in an armchair in Giancarlo's laboratory. Giancarlo, leafing through a bundle of documents in his hands, heaved a long sigh.

'You do lead an interesting life, John. Here, there, everywhere. You've done us a great service tonight. The three men you speak of are indeed the notorious Marzio brothers. Widely supposed to be Sicilians and in the Mafia, but they're not. As you've discovered, they're Corsicans. Corsicans regard the Sicilian Mafiosa as bungling amateurs. Those three have been at the top of our list for years. Never any evidence – but they won't get out of this one. Not when they're found alongside several million francs' worth of heroin. Well, one good turn deserves another.' He handed some papers over to Harlow. 'Jean-Claude has preserved his honour. He broke the code this evening. Interesting reading, no?'

After about a minute Harlow said: 'Yes. A list of Tracchia's and Neubauer's drop-offs throughout Europe.'

'No less.'

'How long to get through to Dunnet?'

Giancarlo looked at him almost pityingly. 'I can reach any place in France inside thirty seconds.'

* * *

There were almost a dozen policemen in the outer office of the police station together with Neubauer and his five felonious companions. Neubauer approached the sergeant at the desk.

'I have been charged. I wish to phone my lawyer. I have the right.'

'You have the right.' The sergeant nodded to the phone on the desk.

'Communications between lawyer and client are privileged.' He indicated an adjacent phone booth. 'I know what that's for. So that the accused can talk to their lawyers. May I?'

The sergeant nodded again.

A phone rang in a rather luxurious flat not half a mile from the police station. Tracchia was reclining at his ease on a couch in the lounge. Beside him was a luscious brunette who evinced a powerful aversion to wearing too many clothes. Tracchia scowled, picked the phone up and said: 'My dear Willi! I am desolate. I was unavoidably detained – '

Neubauer's voice carried clearly.

'Are you alone?'

'No.'

'Then be alone.'

Tracchia said to the girl: 'Georgette, my dear, go powder your nose.' She rose, sulkily, and left the room. Into the phone he said: 'Clear now.'

'You can thank your lucky stars that you were unavoidably detained otherwise you'd be where I am now – on the way to prison. Now listen.'

Tracchia listened very intently indeed, his normally handsome face ugly in anger as Neubauer gave a brief account of what had happened. He finished by saying: 'So. Take the Lee Enfield and binoculars. If he gets there first pick him off when he comes ashore – if he survives Pauli's attentions. If you get there first, go aboard and wait for him. Then lose the gun in the water. Who's aboard *The Chevalier* now?'

'Just Pauli. I'll take Yonnie with me. I may need a lookout or signal-man. And look, Willi, not to worry. You'll be sprung tomorrow. Associating with criminals is not a crime in itself and there's not a single shred of evidence against you.'

'How can we be sure? How can you be sure that you yourself are in the clear? I wouldn't put anything beyond that bastard Harlow. Just get him for me.'

'That, Willi, will be a pleasure.'

Harlow was on the phone in Giancarlo's laboratory. He said: 'So. Simultaneous arrests 5 a.m. tomorrow. There's going to be an awful lot of unhappy people in Europe by 5.10 a.m. I'm in a bit of a hurry so I'll leave Giancarlo to give you all thc details. Hope to see you later tonight. Meantime, I have an appointment.'

CHAPTER ELEVEN

Rory said: 'Mr Harlow, are you secret service or special agent or something?'

Harlow glanced at him, then returned his eyes to the road. He was driving quickly but nowhere near his limit: there seemed to be no compelling urgency about the task on hand. He said: 'I'm an out of work race driver.'

'Come on. Who are you kidding?'

'No one. In your own phraseology, Rory, just giving Mr Dunnet a bit of a hand, like.'

'Doing what, Mr Harlow? I mean, Mr Dunnet doesn't seem to be doing very much, does he?'

'Mr Dunnet is a co-ordinator. I suppose I'm what might be called his field man.'

'Yes. But doing *what*?'

'Investigating other Grand Prix drivers. Keeping an eye on them, rather. And mechanics – anyone connected with racing.'

'I see.' Rory, clearly, did not see at all. 'I'm not being rude, Mr Harlow, but why pick you? Why not investigate you?'

'A fair question. Probably because I've been so very lucky in the last two years or so that they figured that I was making more money honestly than I possibly could dishonestly.'

'That figures.' Rory was in a very judicial mood. 'But *why* were you investigating?'

'Because something has been smelling and smelling badly on the Grand Prix circuits for over a year now. Cars were losing that seemed a certainty to win. Cars were winning that shouldn't have had a chance. Cars had mysterious accidents. Cars went off the track where there was no earthly reason why they should have gone off the track. They ran out of petrol when they shouldn't have run out of petrol. Engines over-heated through a mysterious loss of oil or coolant or both. Drivers fell ill at the most mysterious times – and the most inconvenient times. And as there is so much prestige, pride, power and above all profit in running a highly successful racing car, it was at first thought that a manufacturer or, more likely, a race team owner was trying to corner the market for himself.'

'But he wasn't?'

'As you so brightly remark, he wasn't. This became clear when manufacturers and team owners discovered that they were *all* being victimized. They approached Scotland Yard only to be told that they were powerless to intervene. The Yard called in Interpol. In effect, Mr Dunnet.'

'But how did you get on to people like Tracchia and Neubauer?'

'In the main, illegally. Round the clock telephone switchboard watch, maximum surveillance of all suspects at every Grand Prix meeting and interception of all incoming and out-going mail. We found five drivers and seven or eight mechanics who were stashing away more money than they could have possibly earned. But it was an irregular sort of thing for most of them. It's impossible to fix every race. But Tracchia and Neubauer were stashing it away after every race. So we figured they were selling something – and there's only one thing you can sell for the kind of money they were getting.'

'Drugs. Heroin.'

'Indeed.' He pointed ahead and Rory caught the sign 'BANDOL' picked up by the headlights. Harlow slowed, lowered his window, poked his head out and looked up. Bands of cloud were beginning to spread across the sky but there was still much more starlit sky than cloud. Harlow withdrew his head and said: 'We could have picked a better night for the job. Far too damn bright. They're bound to have a guard, maybe two, for your mother. Point is, will they be keeping a watch – not only seeing that your mother doesn't escape but that no one comes aboard? No reason *why* they should assume that anyone should try to board *The Chevalier* – I can't think of any way they can have heard of the misfortune that has happened to Neubauer and his pals. But that's the way an organization like the Marzio brothers has survived so long – by never taking chances.'

'So we assume there is a guard, Mr Harlow?'

'That is what we assume.'

Harlow drove into the little town, parked the car in an empty high-walled builder's yard where it could not possibly be seen from the narrow alleyway outside. They left the car and soon, keeping in deep shadow, were cautiously picking their way along the small waterfront and harbour. They halted and scanned the bay to the east.

'Isn't that her?' Although there was no one within earshot, Rory's voice was a tense whisper. 'Isn't that her?'

'*The Chevalier* for sure.'

There were at least a dozen yachts and cruisers anchored in the brilliantly moonlit and almost mirror-smooth little bay. The one nearest the shore was a rather splendid motor yacht, nearer fifty feet than forty, and had very definitely a blue hull and white topsides.

'And now?' Rory said. 'What do we do now?' He was shivering, not because of cold or, as had been the case in the Villa Hermitage, of apprehension, but because of sheer excitement. Harlow glanced thoughtfully upwards. The sky was still heavily overcast although there was a bar of cloud moving in the direction of the moon.

'Eat. I'm hungry.'

'Eat? Eat? But-but, I mean – ' Rory gestured towards the yacht.

'All things in their time. Your mother's hardly likely to vanish in the next hour. Besides, if we were to – ah – borrow a boat and go out to *The Chevalier* . . . I don't much fancy being picked out in this brilliant moonlight. There are clouds moving across. Let's bide a wee.'

'Let's what?'

'An old Scottish phrase. Let's wait a little while *Festina lente.*'

Rory looked at him in bafflement. '*Festina* what?'

'You really are an ignorant young layabout.' Harlow smiled to rob his words of offence. 'An even older Latin phrase. Make haste slowly.'

They moved away and brought up at a waterside café which Harlow inspected from the outside. He shook his head and they walked on to a second café, where the same thing happened. The third café they entered. It was three-parts empty. They took seats by a curtained window.

Rory said: 'What's this place got that the others haven't?'

Harlow twitched back the curtain. 'A view.' Their vantage point commanded an excellent view of *The Chevalier.*

'I see.' Rory consulted his menu without enthusiasm. 'I can't eat a thing.'

Harlow said encouragingly: 'Let's try a little something.'

Five minutes later two enormous dishes of bouillabaisse were set before them. Five minutes after that Rory's dish was completely empty. Harlow smiled at both the empty plate and Rory, then his smile abruptly vanished.

'Rory. Look at me. Don't look elsewhere. Especially don't look at the bar. Act and speak naturally. Bloke's just come in whom I used to know very slightly. A mechanic who left the Coronado team a few weeks after I joined. Your father fired him for theft. He was very friendly with Tracchia and from the fact that he's in Bandol it's a million to one that he still is.'

A small dark man in brown overalls, so lean and scrawny as to be almost wizened, sat at the bar with a full glass of beer before him. He took his first sip of it and as he did so his eyes strayed to the mirror at the back of the bar. He could clearly see Harlow talking earnestly to Rory. He spluttered and half-choked over his beer. He lowered his glass, put coins on the counter and left as unobtrusively as possible.

Harlow said: '"Yonnie" they used to call him. I don't know his real name. I think he's certain we neither saw nor recognized him. If he's with Tracchia, and he must be, this makes it for sure that Tracchia is already aboard. Either Tracchia's temporarily relieved him of guard duties so that he could come ashore for a much-needed drink or Tracchia's sent him away because he doesn't want any witnesses around when he picks me off when I go out to the boat.'

Harlow pulled back the curtains and they both looked out. They could see a small outboard-powered dinghy heading directly towards *The Chevalier.* Rory looked questioningly at Harlow.

Harlow said: 'Our Nicolo Tracchia is an impulsive, not to say impetuous lad, which is why he's not quite the driver he could be. Five minutes from now he'll be in the shadows somewhere outside waiting to gun me down the moment I step out of here. Run up to the car, Rory. Bring me some of that twine – and adhesive tape. I think we may need it. Meet me about fifty yards along the quay there, at the head of the landing steps.'

As Harlow signalled the waiter for his bill, Rory left, walking with some degree of restraint. As soon as he had passed through the bead-curtained doorway he broke into a dead run. Arrived at the Ferrari, he opened the boot, stuffed twine and tape into his pockets, closed the boot, hesitated, then opened the driver's door and pulled out the four automatics from under the seat. He selected the smallest, pushed the other three back into concealment, studied the one he held in his hand, eased the safety catch off, looked guiltily around and stuffed the automatic into an inside pocket. He made his way quickly down to the waterfront.

Near the top of the landing steps was a double row of barrels, stacked two high. Harlow and Rory stood silently in the shadow, the former with a gun in his hand. They could both see and hear the outboard dinghy approaching. The engine slowed, then cut out: there came the sound of feet mounting the wooden landing steps, then two figures; appeared on the quay, Tracchia and Yonnie: Tracchia was carrying a rifle. Harlow moved out from the shadows.

'Keep quite still,' he said. 'Tracchia, that gun on the ground. Hands high and turn your backs to me. I get tired of repeating myself but the first of you to make the slightest suspicious movement will be shot through the back of the head. At four feet I am not likely to miss. Rory, see what your former friend and his friend are carrying.'

Rory's search produced two guns.

'Throw them in the water. Come on, you two. Behind those barrels. Face down, hands behind your backs. Rory, attend to our friend Yonnie.'

With the expertise born of recent and intensive practice Rory had Yonnie trussed like a turkey in less than two minutes.

Harlow said: 'You know what the tape is for?'

Rory knew what the tape was for. He used about a couple of feet of black insulated adhesive tape that effectively ensured Yonnie's total silence.

Harlow said: 'Can he breathe?'

'Just.'

'"Just" is enough. Not that it matters. We'll leave him here. Maybe someone will find him in the morning. Not that that matters either. Up, Tracchia.'

'But aren't you – '

'Mr Tracchia we need. Who's to say there isn't another guard aboard? Tracchia here is a specialist in hostages so he'll know what we want him for.'

Rory looked up at the sky. 'That cloud that's moving towards the moon is taking its time about it.'

'It doesn't appear to be in any great hurry about it. But we'll take a chance on it. We have our life assurance with us.'

The outboard motor dinghy moved across the moonlit water. Traccia was at the controls while Harlow, gun in hand, sat amidships facing him. Rory was in the bows, facing forward. At this point, the blue and white yacht was only a hundred yards away.

In the wheelhouse of the yacht a tall and powerfully built man had a pair of binoculars to his eyes. His face tightened. He laid down the binoculars, took a gun from a drawer, left the wheel-house, climbed the ladder there and spreadeagled himself on the cabin roof.

The dinghy came alongside the water-skiing steps at the stern and Rory made fast. At a gesture from Harlow, Tracchia climbed the ladder first and moved back slowly as Harlow, the gun trained on him, climbed the steps in turn. Rory followed. Harlow made a gesture that Rory should remain where he was, thrust his gun in Tracchia's back and moved off to search the boat.

One minute later Harlow, Rory and a blackly scowling Tracchia were in *The Chevalier's* brightly lit saloon.

Harlow said: 'No one aboard, it seems. I take it that Mrs MacAlpine is behind that locked door below. I want the key, Tracchia.'

A deep voice said: 'Stand still. Don't turn round. Drop that gun.'

Harlow stood still, didn't turn round and dropped his gun. The seaman walked into the saloon from the after door.

Tracchia smiled, almost beatifically. 'That was well done, Pauli.'

'My pleasure, Signor Tracchia.' He passed by Rory, gave him a contemptuous shove that sent him reeling into a corner of the settee and moved forward to pick up Harlow's gun.

'You drop *your* gun. Now!' Rory's voice had a most distinct quaver to it.

Pauli swung around, an expression of total astonishment on his face. Rory had a gun clutched in two very unsteady hands.

Pauli smiled broadly. 'Well, well, well. What a brave little gamecock.' He brought up his gun.

Rory's hands and arms were trembling like an aspen leaf in an autumn gale. He compressed his lips, screwed his eyes shut and pulled the trigger. In that confined space the report of the gun was deafening but even so not loud enough to drown out Pauli's shout of agony. Pauli stared down in stupefaction as the blood from his shattered right shoulder seeped down between the clutching fingers of his left hand. Tracchia, too, wore a similarly bemused expression, one that changed to one of considerable pain as Harlow's vicious swinging left hook sank deeply into his stomach. He bent double, Harlow struck him on the back of the neck but Tracchia was tough and durable. Still bent almost double, he staggered through the after door out on to the deck. As he did so, he passed Rory, very pale and looking very faint and clearly through with shooting exploits for the night. It was as well. Harlow was in such close pursuit that he might well have been the victim of Rory's extremely wobbly marksmanship.

Rory looked at the wounded Pauli then at the two guns lying at his feet. Rory rose and pointed his gun at Pauli. He said: 'Sit down.'

Pain-wracked though he was, Pauli moved with alacrity to obey. There was no saying where Rory's next unpredictable shot might lodge itself. As he moved to a corner of the saloon the sound of blows and grunts of pain could be clearly heard from outside. Rory scooped up the two guns and ran through the after door.

On deck, the fight had clearly reached its climax. Tracchia, his wildly flailing feet clear of the deck and his body arched like a bow, had his back on the guardrail and the upper half of his body over the water. Harlow's hands were on his throat. Tracchia, in turn, was belabouring Harlow's already sadly battered and bruised face, but the belabouring was of no avail. Harlow, his face implacable, pushed him farther and farther out. Suddenly changing his tactics, he removed his right hand from Tracchia's throat, hooked it under his thighs and proceeded to tip him over the guard-rail. When Tracchia spoke, his voice came as a wholly understandable croak.

'I can't swim! I can't swim!'

If Harlow had heard him there was not even the most minuscule change of expression on his face to register that fact. He gave a final convulsive heave, the flailing legs disappeared and Tracchia entered the water with a resounding splash that threw water as high as Harlow's face. A barred cloud had at last crossed the moon. Harlow gazed down intently into the water for about fifteen seconds, produced his torch and made a complete circuit of the water around the yacht until he arrived back at his starting place. Again, still breathing deeply and quickly, he peered over the side, then turned to Rory. He said: 'Maybe he was right at that. Maybe he can't swim.'

Rory tore off his jacket. 'I can swim. I'm a very good swimmer, Mr Harlow.'

Harlow's iron hand grabbed him by the collar of his shirt. 'You, Rory, are out of your mind.'

Rory looked at him for a long moment, nodded, picked up his jacket and put it on again. He said: 'Vermin?'

'Yes.' They went back into the saloon. Pauli was still huddled in a settee, moaning. Harlow said: 'The key to Mrs MacAlpine's cabin.'

Pauli nodded in the direction of a cabinet drawer. Harlow found the key, removed the first-aid box from its clip on the bulkhead, ushered Pauli below at the point of his gun, opened the first cabin door, gestured Pauli inside and threw in the first-aid box. He said: 'I'll have a doctor here within half an hour. Meantime, I don't care a damn whether you live or die.' He left and locked the cabin door from the outside.

In the next cabin, a woman of about forty sat on a stool by her bunk. Pale and thin from her long confinement, she was still quite beautiful. The resemblance to her daughter was startling. She was listless, totally apathetic, the epitome of resignation and despair. The sound of the gun and the commotion on the upper deck could not have gone unregistered, but no signs of registration showed in her face.

A key turned in the lock, the door opened and Harlow came in. She made no move. He walked to within three feet of her and still she gazed uncaringly downwards.'

Harlow touched her shoulder and said, very gently: 'I've come to take you home, Marie.'

She turned her head in slow and unbelieving wonderment, initially and understandably not recognizing the battered face before her. Then, slowly, almost incredulously, recognition dawned upon her. She rose unsteadily to her feet, half smiled at him, then tremblingly took a step forward, put her thin arms around his neck and buried her face in his shoulder.

'Johnny Harlow,' she whispered. 'My dear, dear Johnny. Johnny Harlow. What have they done to your face?'

'Nothing that time won't cure,' Harlow said briskly. 'After all, it wasn't all that hot to begin with.' He patted her back as if to reassure her of his actual presence, then gently disengaged himself. 'I think there's someone else who would like to see you, Marie.'

For someone who claimed that he could not swim, Tracchia was cleaving through the water like a torpedo. He reached the landing steps, scrambled up to the quay, and headed for the nearest phone booth. He put through a reverse charge call to Vignolles and had to stand there for almost five minutes before his call came through: the French telephone service is not world renowned. He asked for Jacobson and finally reached him in his bedroom. Tracchia's account of the evening's happenings were succinct and to the point but could have been shorter as it was heavily burdened with a wide range of expletives. 'So that's it, Jake,' Tracchia finished up. 'That bastard has outsmarted us all'

Jacobson's face, as he sat on his bed, was tight with anger but he was clearly in control of himself. He said: 'Not quite yet. So we've lost our ace in the hole. We'll just have to get ourselves another one, won't we? You understand? Meet you at Bandol inside the hour. Usual place.'

'Passport?'

'Yes.'

'In my bedside table drawer. And for Christ's sake bring me a set of dry clothing or I'll have pneumonia before the night is out.'

Tracchia emerged from the phone booth. He was actually smiling. He went to take up position among some crates and barrels, seeking a safe position where he could keep *The Chevalier* under observation and, in the process of doing so, literally tripped over the prostrate Yonnie.

'Good God, Yonnie, I'd forgotten just where you were.' The bound and gagged man looked up with pleading eyes. Tracchia shook his head. 'Sorry, can't untie you yet. That bastard Harlow, young MacAlpine rather, has shot Pauli, I had to swim for it. The two of them will be coming ashore any minute. Harlow may check whether you're still here. If he does, and you're gone, he'll raise a hue and cry immediately: if you're still here he'll reckon that you can be left in cold storage for a while. Gives us more time to play with. When they've landed and gone take the dinghy out to *The Chevalier*. Find a bag and stuff it with all the papers in the two top drawers of the chart-table. God, if the police were ever to lay hands on that lot! Among other things, your days would be numbered. You'll take them to your place in Marseilles in my car and wait there. If you get those papers you're in the clear. Harlow didn't recognize you, it was too dark in the shadows here, nobody even knows your name. Understand?'

Yonnie nodded glumly then turned his head in the direction of the harbour. Tracchia nodded. The sound of the outboard was unmistakable and soon the dinghy appeared in sight round the bows of *The Chevalier.* Tracchia prudently withdrew twenty or thirty yards along the waterfront. The dinghy came alongside the landing steps and Rory was the first out, painter in hand. As he secured the dinghy, Harlow helped Marie ashore, then followed himself, her suitcase in his hand. His gun was in his other hand. Tracchia toyed briefly with the idea of way-laying Harlow in the shadows but almost immediately and very prudently changed his mind. He knew that Harlow would be in no mood to be taking any chances and, if necessary, would shoot and shoot to kill without the slightest compunction.

Harlow came straight to where Yonnie lay, bent over him, straightened, and said: 'He'll keep.' The three crossed the road to the nearest phone booth – the one that Tracchia had lately occupied – and Harlow went inside. Tracchia moved stealthily along behind the cover of barrels and crates until he reached Yonnie. He produced a knife and cut him free. Yonnie sat up and he had the expression of a man who would have given a great deal to be able to shout in pain. He rubbed hands and wrists in agony: Rory was no respecter of circulations. By and by, gingerly and clearly not enjoying the process, he removed the insulated tape from his face. He opened his mouth but Tracchia clapped his hand across it to prevent what would be doubtless a torrential outpouring of imprecations.

'Quiet,' Tracchia whispered. 'They're just on the other side of the road. Harlow's in the phone booth.' He removed his hand. 'When they leave, I'm going to follow them to see that they do really leave Bandol. As soon as they're out of sight, get down to the dinghy. Use the oars. We don't want Harlow hearing the outboard start up and coming back to investigate.'

'Me? Row?' Yonnie said huskily. He flexed his fingers and winced. 'My hands are dead.'

'You'd better get them back to life fast,' Tracchia said unfeelingly. 'Or *you're* going to be dead. Ah, now.' He lowered his voice still further. 'He's just left the phone box. Be dead quiet. That bastard Harlow can hear a leaf drop twenty feet away.'

Harlow, Rory and Mrs MacAlpine walked up a street away from the waterfront. They turned a corner and disappeared. Tracchia said: 'Get going.'

He watched Yonnie head for the landing steps then followed quickly after the trio in front. For about three minutes he trailed them at a very discreet distance indeed, then lost sight of them as they turned another left corner. He peered cautiously round the corner, saw that it was a cul-de-sac, hesitated and then stiffened as he heard the unmistakable sound of a Ferrari engine starting up. Shivering violently in his still soaking clothes, he pressed himself into the darkness of a recessed and unlit alleyway. The Ferrari emerged from the cul-de-sac, turned left and headed north out of Bandol. Tracchia watched it go then hurried back to the phone booth.

There was the usual frustrating delay in getting through to Vignolles. Eventually, he succeeded in reaching Jacobson. He said: 'Harlow's just left with Rory and Mrs MacAlpine. He made a phone call before he left – almost certainly to Vignolles to tell MacAlpine that he's got his wife back. I'd leave by the back door if I were you.'

'No worry,' Jacobson sounded confident. 'I am leaving by the back door. The fire-escape. I've already got our cases in the Aston and our passports in my pocket. I'm now on my way to collect our third passport. See you.'

Tracchia replaced the receiver. He was about to open the booth door when he stopped and stood as if a man turned to stone. A large black Citroën had slid silently down to the waterfront, showing only side-lights. Even those were switched off before the car came to a halt. No flashing lights, no howling sirens – but it was indisputably a police car and one paying a very private visit. Four uniformed policemen came out of the car. Tracchia pried open the door of the booth so that the automatic light went out, then leaned as far back as possible, praying that he wouldn't be seen. He wasn't. The four policemen at once disappeared behind the barrels where Yonnie had been, two of them with lit torches in hand, and reappeared within ten seconds, one of them carrying some unidentifiable objects in his hand. Tracchia did not need to see it to know what the man was carrying – the twine and black tape that had immobilized and silenced Yonnie. The four policemen held a brief conference then headed for the landing steps. Twenty seconds later a rowing boat was heading purposefully but silently towards *The Chevalier.*

Tracchia emerged from the booth, fists clenched, his face black with anger and softly but audibly swearing to himself. The only printable word, and one that was repeated many times, was 'Harlow'. The bitter realization had come to Tracchia that Harlow had not phoned Vignolles: he had phoned the local police.

In her room in Vignolles Mary was getting ready for dinner when a knock came at her door. She opened it to find Jacobson standing there. He said: 'Can I have a private word with you, Mary? It's very important.'

She regarded him with mild astonishment then opened the door for him to enter. Jacobson closed the door behind him.

She said curiously: 'What's so important? What do you want?'

Jacobson pulled a gun from his waist-band. 'You. I'm in trouble and I need some form of security to make sure that I don't get into more trouble.

You're the security. Pack an overnight bag and give me your passport.'

She gave him her passport and packed the bag. Jacobson crossed to the bed and snapped shut the catches of her case. 'You'd better come now.'

'Where are you taking me?'

'Now, I said.' He lifted his gun menacingly.

'Then you'd better shoot me now. Number eight.'

'Cuneo. Then parts beyond.' His voice was harsh but had the ring of sincerity. 'I never make war on women. You'll be released within twenty-four hours.'

'I'll be dead in twenty-four hours.' She picked up her handbag. 'May I go to the bathroom? I feel sick.'

Jacobson opened the bathroom door and looked inside. 'No window. No telephone. OK.'

Mary entered the bathroom and closed the door behind her. She took a pen from her handbag, scribbled a few shaky words on a piece of paper, placed the paper face down on the floor behind the door and left. Jacobson was waiting for her. He had her case in his left hand, a gun in the other. Both gun and right hand were buried deep in his jacket pocket.

On board *The Chevalier,* Yonnie thrust the last of the documents from the chart-table into a large briefcase. He returned to the saloon, placed the briefcase on a settee and went down the companionway to the accommodation quarters. He went to his own cabin and there spent a hurried five minutes in cramming his own most personal possessions into a canvas bag. He then made a tour of the other cabins, rifling the drawers for whatever money or articles of value that he might find. He found a considerable amount, returned to his own cabin and stuffed them inside his bag. He zipped the bag shut and climbed up the companionway. Four steps from the top he stopped. His face should have been masked in disbelief and terror but it wasn't. Yonnie had run out of emotions and the capacity to display them.

Four very large armed policemen were resting comfortably on the settees in the saloon. A sergeant, with the briefcase on his knees, his elbow on the case and a gun in his hand pointing approximately in the direction of Yonnie's heart, said genially: 'Going some place Yonnie?'

CHAPTER TWELVE

Once again, the Ferrari was moving through the darkness. Harlow was not idling but neither was he pushing the car hard. As on the trip from Marseilles to Bandol, it seemed that the need for urgency was not there. Mrs MacAlpine was in the front passenger seat wearing, at Harlow's insistence, a double safety belt. A rather drowsy Rory was stretched out on the back seats,

Harlow said: 'So, you see, it was all quite simple, really. Jacobson was the master-mind behind this particular operation. It will turn out that the Marzio brothers were the ones that really mattered. Anyway, it was Jacobson's idea to gamble on the Grand Prix drivers and he altered the odds in his favour by suborning no fewer that five drivers. Plus even more mechanics. He paid them plenty – but he made a fortune himself. I was the thorn in his flesh – he knew better than to try to get at me, and as I was winning the majority of the races it was making his business very difficult indeed. So he tried to kill me at Clermont-Ferrand. I have proof – both stills and cine film.'

In the rear Rory stirred sleepily. 'But how could he do that to you while you were on the track?'

'Me? And a lot of others? Two ways. A radio-controlled explosive device on a suspension strut or a chemically operated explosive device on the hydraulic brake lines. Both devices, I imagine, would blow clear on detonation and leave no trace of their presence. Anyway, it's on film record that Jacobson replaced both a strut and a brake line.'

Rory said: 'Which is why he always insisted on being alone when inspecting smashed cars?'

Harlow nodded, temporarily lost in thought. Mrs MacAlpine said: 'But how – how could you degrade yourself in this awful fashion?'

'Well, it wasn't all that pleasant. But you know the blaze of publicity I live in. I couldn't move privately, more or less to brush my teeth, than to do the job I was asked to. I had to take the heat off myself, step out of the limelight and become a loner. It wasn't all that difficult. As for working my way down to the transporter job – well, I *had* to find out whether the stuff was coming from the Coronado garage or not. It was.'

'The stuff?'

'The dust. European jargon for heroin. My dear Marie, there are more ways to dusty death than losing control on a Grand Prix race-track.'

'The way to dusty death.' She shivered and repeated the words. 'The way to dusty death. Did James know about this, Johnny?'

'He knew six months ago that the transporter was being used – oddly enough, he never suspected Jacobson. They'd been together too long, I suppose. Some way, any way, they had to have the price of his silence. You were that price. And for good measure he was also being blackmailed for approximately twenty-five thousand pounds a month.'

She was silent for almost a minute then she said: 'Did James know I was still alive?'

'Yes.'

'But he knew about the heroin – all those months he knew. Think of all those people ruined, perhaps dead. Think of all – '

Harlow reached out his right hand and caught her left in his. 'I think, Marie, that perhaps he loves you.'

A car approached then, headlights dipped. Harlow dipped his. Briefly, as if by mistake, the approaching car's headlights came on full beam, then dipped again. As they passed each other, the driver of the other car turned to his passenger, a girl with her hands bound in front of her.

'Tut! Tut! Tut!' Jacobson sounded in almost high humour. 'Young Lochinvar headed in the wrong direction.'

In the Ferrari Mrs MacAlpine said: 'And James will have to stand trial for his – complicity in this heroin traffic?'

'James will never stand trial for anything.'

'But heroin – '

Harlow said: 'Heroin? Heroin? Rory, did you hear anyone mentioning the word "heroin"?'

'Mother's been through a pretty rough time, Mr Harlow. I think she is beginning to imagine things.'

The Aston Martin pulled up outside a darkened café on the outskirts of Bandol. A violently shivering Tracchia emerged from the shadows and climbed into the back of the Aston Martin.

He said: 'Complete with insurance policy, I see. Now, for God's sake, Jake, stop at the first clump of trees outside Bandol. Unless I change out of these clothes damn quick I'm going to freeze to death.'

'Right. Where's Yonnie?'

'In gaol'

'Jesus!' Even the abnormally phlegmatic Jacobson was shaken. 'What in the hell happened?'

'I'd sent Yonnie out in the dinghy while I was phoning you. I'd told him to bring ashore all the papers and documents in the two top drawers in the chart-table. You know how important those are, Jake?'

'I know.' There was no disguising die harsh edge of strain in Jacobson's voice.

'Remember I'd told you that I thought Harlow had phoned Vignolles? He hadn't. The bastard had phoned the Bandol police. They arrived while I was still in the phone booth. There was nothing I could do. They rowed out to *The Chevalier* and nabbed him there.'

'And the papers?'

'One of the police was carrying a large attaché case.'

'I don't think that Bandol is a very healthy place for us to be.' Jacobson was back on balance again. He drove off but not in a fashion ostentatious enough to attract attention. As they reached the outskirts of the town, he said: 'That's it, then. What with those papers and that cassette the whole operation's blown. *Termine. Fine.* The end of the road.' He seemed remarkably calm.

'And now?'

'Operation fly-away. I've had it planned for months. First stop is our flat in Cuneo.'

'Nobody knows about it?'

'Nobody. Except Willi. And he won't talk. Besides, it's not under our names anyway.' He pulled up alongside a thicket of trees. 'The boot's unlocked and the grey case is yours. Those clothes you're wearing – leave them among the trees.'

'Why? It's a perfectly good suit and – '

'What's' going to happen if the Customs search us and find a suit of soaking wet clothes?'

'You have a point,' Tracchia said and got out of the car. When he returned in two or three minutes, Jacobson was in the back seat. Tracchia said: 'You want me to drive?'

'We're in a hurry and my name is not Nicolo Tracchia.' As Tracchia engaged gear he went on: 'We should have no trouble with the Customs and police at the Col de Tende. The word won't be out for hours yet. It's quite possible that they haven't discovered that Mary is missing yet. Besides, they've no idea where we're heading. No reason why they should notify border police. But by the time we reach the Swiss frontier we may be in trouble.'

'So?'

'Two hours in Cuneo. We'll switch cars, leave the Aston in the garage and take the Peugeot. Pack some more clothes for ourselves, pick up our other passports and identification papers, then call in Erita and our photographer friend. Within the hour Erita will have turned our Mary into a blonde and very shortly afterwards our friend will have a nice shiny British passport for her. Then we drive up to Switzerland. If the word is out, then the border boys will be on the alert. Well, as alert as those cretins can be in the middle of the night. But they'll be looking for an Aston Martin with one man and a brunette inside – that's assuming our friends back in Vignolles have managed to put two and two together, which I very much doubt. But they won't be looking for two men and blonde in a Peugeot, with passports carrying completely different names.'

Tracchia was now driving the car close to its limits and he had almost to shout to make himself heard. The Aston Martin is a magnificent machine but not particularly renowned for the quietness of its engine: there were carping critics who occasionally maintained that the engines for the David Brown tractor division found their way into the wrong machines. Ferrari and Lamborghini owners had been known to describe it as the fastest lorry in Europe. Tracchia said: 'You sound very sure of yourself, Jake.'

'I am.'

Tracchia glanced at the girl by his side. 'And Mary here? God knows we're no angels but I don't want any harm to come to her.'

'No harm. I told her I don't make war on women and I'll keep my word on that. She's our safe conduct if the police come after us.'

'Or Johnny Harlow?'

'Or Harlow. When we get to Zurich, each of us will go to the bank in turns, cash and transfer money while the others keeps her as hostage. Then we fly out into the wild blue yonder,'

'You expect trouble in Zurich?'

'None. We haven't even been arrested far less convicted so our Zurich friends won't open up. Besides, we're under different names and with numbered accounts.'

'The wild blue yonder? With teleprinted copies of our photographs at every airport in the world?'

'Only the major ones on scheduled flights. Lots of minor airfields around. There's a private flight division in Kloten airport and I have a pilot friend there. He'll file a flight plan for Geneva which will mean that we don't have to pass customs. We'll land somewhere quite a way from Switzerland. He can always claim that he was hi-jacked. Ten thousand Swiss francs should fit it.'

'You think of everything, don't you, Jake?' There was genuine admiration in Tracchia's voice.

'I try.' Jacobson, uncharacteristically, sounded almost complacent. 'I try.'

The red Ferrari was drawn up outside the chalet in Vignolles. MacAlpine held his sobbing wife in his arms but he was not looking as happy as he might have done in the circumstances. Dunnet approached Harlow.

'How do you feel, boy?'

'Bloody well exhausted.'

'I've bad news, Johnny. Jacobson's gone.'

'He can wait. I'll get him.'

'There's more to it than that, Johnny.'

'What?'

'He's taken Mary with him.'

Harlow stood immobile, his drawn and weary face without expression. He said: 'Does James know?'

'I've just told him. And I think he's just telling his wife.' He handed a note to Harlow. 'I found this in Mary's bathroom.'

Harlow looked at it. '"Jacobson is taking me to Cuneo."' Without even a pause he said: 'I'll go now.'

'You can't, man! You're totally exhausted. You said so yourself.'

'Not any more. Come with me?'

Dunnet accepted the inevitable. 'You stop me. But I've no gun.'

'Guns we have,' Rory said. He produced four as proof of his assertion.

'We?' Harlow said. 'You're not coming.'

'I would remind you, Mr Harlow,' Rory said with some asperity, 'that I saved your life twice tonight. All good things come in threes. I have the right.'

Harlow nodded. 'You have the right.'

MacAlpine and his wife were staring numbly at them. The expressions on their faces were an extraordinary combination of happiness and a broken bewilderment.

MacAlpine said, tears in his eyes: 'Alexis has told me everything. I'll never be able to thank you, I'll never be able to forgive myself and the rest of my life will be too short for the apologies I have to make to you. You destroyed your career, ruined yourself, to bring my Marie back.'

'Ruined me?' Harlow said calmly. 'Nonsense. There's another season coming up.' He smiled without mirth. 'And there'll be a fair bit of the top-flight opposition missing.' He smiled again, this time encouragingly. 'I'll bring Mary back. With your help, James. Everybody knows you. You know everybody and you're a millionaire. There's only one way from here to Cuneo. Phone someone, preferably some big trucking firm in Nice. Offer them £10,000 to block the French end of the Col de Tende. My passport's gone. You understand?'

'I've a friend in Nice who would do it for nothing. But what's the use, Johnny? It's a job for the police.'

'No. And I'm not thinking about the continental habit of first of all riddling wanted cars and then asking the dead bodies questions. What I – '

'Johnny, whether you or the police get to them first makes no difference. I know now that you know everything, have known for a long time. Those are the two men who will bring me down.'

Harlow said mildly: 'There's a third man, James. Willi Neubauer. But he'll never talk. Admission to kidnapping would bring him another ten years in prison. You weren't listening to me, James. Phone Nice. Phone Nice now. All I said was that I would bring Mary back.'

MacAlpine and his wife stood together, listening to the howl of the Ferrari engine die away in the distance. In what was almost a whisper, Marie MacAlpine said: 'What did that mean, James? "All I said is that I would bring Mary back."'

'I've got to phone Nice and at once. Then the biggest drink the château can offer, a small dinner then bed. There's nothing more we can do now.' He paused, then went on almost sadly: 'I have my limitations. I do not operate in Johnny Harlow's class.'

'What did he mean, James?'

'What he said.' MacAlpine tightened his arm around his wife's shoulder. 'He brought you back, didn't he? He'll bring our Mary back. Don't you know they're in love?'

'What did he mean, James?'

MacAlpine said in a dead voice: 'He meant that neither of us would ever see Jacobson and Tracchia again.'

The nightmare journey to the Col de Tende, a journey that would live in the minds of Dunnet and Rory for ever, was conducted, with only one exception, in absolute conversational silence, partially because Harlow was completely concentrated on the job on hand, partially because both Dunnet and Rory had been reduced to a state pretty close to abject terror. Harlow was not only driving the Ferrari to its limits – in the opinions of his two passengers he was driving it far beyond its limits. As they drove along the autoroute between Cannes and Nice, Dunnet looked at the speedometer. It read 260 kph – something over 160 miles per hour.

He said: 'May I say something?'

For a flicker of a second Harlow glanced at him. 'But of course.'

'Jesus Christ Almighty. Superstar, if you want. The best driver in the world, like enough the best driver who's ever lived. But in all bloody hell – '

'Language,' Harlow said mildly. 'My young future brother-in-law is sitting behind us.'

'This is the way you earn a living?'

'Well, yes.' While the seat-belted Dunnet clung in desperate apprehension to any available hand-hold, Harlow braked, changed down, and with all four wheels in a screaming slide and at just under a hundred miles an hour, rounded a corner that few other drivers, however competent, would have attempted at seventy. 'But you must admit it's better than working.'

'Jesus!' Dunnet lapsed into a semi-stunned silence and closed his eyes like a man in prayer. Very probably he was.

The N204, the road between Nice and La Giandola, where it links up with the road from Ventimiglia, is a very winding one, with some spectacular hairpins and rising in places to over three thousand feet, but Harlow treated it all as if he were driving along the autoroute. Presently, both Dunnet and Rory had their eyes closed: it could have been exhaustion but, more likely, they didn't want to see what was going on.

The road was entirely empty. They crossed over the Col de Braus, went through Sospel at a ludicrously illegal speed, passed through the Col de Brouis and reached La Giandola without having met a single car, which was perhaps just as well for the nerves of any driver who might have been coming the other way. Then they went north through Saorge, Fontan and finally the township of Tende itself. It was just beyond Tende that Dunnet stirred and opened his eyes.

He said: 'Am I still alive?'

'I think so.'

Dunnet rubbed his eyes. 'What was that you just said about your brother-in-law?'

'"Just" was a long time ago.' Harlow pondered. 'Looks as if someone has to look after the MacAlpine family. I might as well make it official.'

'You secretive so-and-so. Engaged?'

'Well, no. I haven't asked her yet. And I have news for you, Alexis. You're going to drive this car back to Vignolles while I sleep the sleep of the just. In the back seat. With Mary.'

'You haven't even asked her yet and you're certain you're going to get her back.' Dunnet looked at Harlow in disbelief and shook his head. 'You, Johnny Harlow, are the most arrogant human being I've ever known.'

'Don't you knock my future brother-in-law, Mr Dunnet,' Rory said sleepily from the back. 'By the way, Mr Harlow, if I *am* going to be your brother-in-law, can I call you Johnny?'

Harlow smiled. 'You can call me anything you like. Just as long as it's said in a tone of proper respect.'

'Yes, Mr Harlow. Johnny, I mean.' Suddenly his voice was no longer sleepy. 'Do you see what I see?'

Ahead of them were the headlights of a car negotiating the vicious hairpins of the lower end of the Col de Tende.

'I've been seeing it for quite some time. Tracchia.'

Dunnet looked at him. 'How can you tell?'

'Two things.' Harlow dropped two gears as he approached the first hairpin. 'There aren't half a dozen people in Europe who can drive a car the way that car is being driven.' He dropped another gear and slid round the hairpin with all the calm relaxation of a man sitting in a pew in a church. 'Show an art expert fifty different paintings, and he'll immediately tell you who the artist is. I'm not talking about anything so wildly different as Rembrandt and Renoir. The same school of painters. I can recognize the driving technique of any Grand Prix driver in the world. After all, there are fewer Grand Prix drivers than there are painters. Traccia has the habit of braking slightly early for a corner then accelerating quickly through it.' He threw the Ferrari, tyres shrieking in protest, round the next corner. 'That's Tracchia.'

It was indeed Tracchia. Seated beside him, Jacobson was peering anxiously through the rear window. He said: 'There's someone coming up behind.'

'It's a public road. Anyone can use it.'

'Believe me, Nikki, this is not just anyone.'

In the Ferrari, Harlow said: 'I think we better get ready.' He pressed a button and the windows slid down. Then he reached for his gun and placed it beside him. 'And I'll be greatly obliged if neither of you shoot Mary.'

Dunnet said: 'I just hope to hell that tunnel's blocked.' He brought out his own gun.

The tunnel was indeed blocked, completely and solidly blocked. A very large furniture van was jammed diagonally and apparently immovably into its mouth.

The Aston Martin rounded the last hairpin. Tracchia swore bitterly and braked the car to a halt. Both men gazed apprehensively through the rear window. Mary looked too, though with hope, not fear.

Jacobson said: 'Don't tell me that damned truck jammed there is sheer coincidence. Turn the car, Nikki. God, there they are!'

The Ferrari came sliding round the last corner and accelerated towards them. Tracchia tried desperately to turn his car, a manœuvre made more difficult when Harlow, braking heavily, rammed his Ferrari into the side of the Aston. Jacobson had his gun out and was firing at apparent random.

'Jacobson,' Harlow said urgently. 'Not Tracchia. You'll kill Mary.'

Both men leaned out of their windows and fired just as their windscreen smashed and starred. Jacobson ducked low for safety but he ducked too late. He screamed in agony as two bullets lodged in his left shoulder. In the confusion and noise Mary opened the door and jumped out as quickly as her crippled leg would permit her. Neither man, for the moment, even noticed that she was gone.

Tracchia, only the top of his head visible above the windscreen, eventually managed to wrench his car round and clear then accelerated desperately away. Four seconds later, with Dunnet having practically dragged Mary inside, the Ferrari was in pursuit. Harlow, apparently oblivious to the inflicted cuts, had already smashed his fist through the shattered windscreen. Dunnet completed the work with the butt of his pistol.

Not once, but several times, Mary cried out in fear as Harlow took the Ferrari down through the hairpins of the Col de Tende. Rory had his arm round his sister and although he did not voice his fear he was plainly just as terrified as Mary was. Dunnet, firing his gun through the empty space where the windscreen had been, didn't look particularly happy either. Harlow's face was still, implacable. To an observer, it must have appeared that the car was being driven by a maniac, but Harlow was in complete control. To the accompaniment of the sound of tortured tyres and engine bellowing in the lower gears, he descended the Col as no one had ever done before and, assuredly, no one would ever do again. By the sixth hairpin he was only a matter of feet behind the Aston.

'Stop shooting,' Harlow shouted. He had to shout to make himself heard above the sound of an engine at maximum revolutions in bottom gear.

'Why?'

'Because it's not final enough.'

The Aston, now only a car's length ahead, slid desperately round a right-hand hairpin bend. Harlow, instead of braking, accelerated, spun the wheel viciously to the right and the car slid half-way round the corner on all four screaming, skidding tyres, at right-angles to its line of travel only a second previously, apparently completely out of control. But Harlow had judged matters to a hair-raising degree of nicety: the side of the Ferrari smashed fairly and squarely into that of the Aston. The Ferrari, already practically stopped, rebounded into the middle of the curve. The Aston, moving diagonally now and hopelessly unmanageable, slid out towards the edge. Beyond the edge there was a drop of six hundred feet into the darkened and unseen depdis of a ravine below.

Harlow was out of the stopped Ferrari just before the teetering Aston vanished over the side. He was followed almost immediately by the others. They peered over the edge of the road.

The Aston, descending with apparently incredible slowness, turned slowly over and over as it fell. It disappeared into the depths and the darkness of the ravine. There was a brief thunderclap of sound and a great gout of brilliant orange flame that seemed to reach half-way up to where they stood. Then there was only the silence and the darkness.

On the road above, all four stood quiet and still, like people in a trance, then Mary, shuddering, buried her face in Harlow's shoulder. He put his arm around her and continued to gaze down, unseeingly as it seemed, into the hidden depths of the ravine.

Bear Island

Alistair MacLean

As the *Morning Rose* ploughs through wintry Arctic seas towards Bear Island, ship's doctor Christopher Marlowe is kept busy attending to the sea-sick passengers – a film unit who are to make a film so secret that none of them know much about it. Then passengers and crew begin dying under mysterious circumstances, and Marlowe realizes that the *Morning Rose* has a murderer on board.

Once encamped on the island, suspicion shifts from one survivor to another, and still the killing continues. Someone is hell-bent on preventing Marlowe and the others from sharing the dark secret of the island, and what lies beyond the Gates of Pearl. Beset by increasing paranoia within the frightened group, where few are who they claim to be, Marlowe must contend against weather, terrain and ruthless adversaries, as events build up to a brutal climax in the darkness of the Polar night.

'Alistair MacLean is brilliant at building up the tension'
Sunday Mirror

'Edge-of-the-seat stuff . . . MacLean is back in the location he writes about best'
The Times

978-0-00-616434-0

Circus

Alistair MacLean

Bruno Wildermann of the Wrinfield Circus is the world's greatest trapeze artist, a clairvoyant with near-supernatural powers and an implacable enemy of the East European regime that arrested his family and murdered his wife. The CIA needs such a man, and recruits Bruno for an impossible raid – on the impregnable Lubylan fortress, where his family is held.

Under cover of a circus tour, Bruno prepares to return to his homeland. But before the journey even begins a murderer strikes twice. Somewhere in the circus there is a communist agent with orders to stop Bruno at any cost . . .

Great reading' *Sunday Telegraph*

'An action-packed story . . . finger-biting suspense' *BBC*

978-0-00-616735-8